THANK YOU FOR STARING INTO THE VOID, YOUR SCREAM IS IMPORTANT TO US

I0591107

SHORT STORIES by
RICHARD GADZ

~~████████~~ *n.* **1.** horror induced by
the realisation that it is already too late
to correct a serious mistake or decision.
2. a dread of what is to come; a rational state
of existential fear caused by anticipation
of near-certain future events.

The right of Richard Gadz to be identified as the author of this work
has been asserted by him in accordance with the Copyright Designs
& Patents Act 1988

ISBN 978-0-9565049-8-2

First Printing, 2025

THANK YOU FOR STARING INTO THE VOID, YOUR SCREAM IS IMPORTANT TO US

SHORT STORIES

CONTENTS

The king did not like to be kept waiting. Entertainment had been promised, and sitting here waiting was not, in his opinion, entertaining. The queen didn't like waiting either, and nor did the three little princes, who ran about the ballroom ignored by their parents but eyed carefully by the stiffly attendant servants and the neatly arranged ranks of courtiers. The princes sped across the herringboned wooden floor as they scrambled around the thrones, under the courtiers' chairs, over the hems of the female courtiers' skirts. Their gleeful chattering echoed off the vaulted ceiling and vanished into the red, flowing draperies on the walls. Outside the castle, a storm was brewing.

The king's wrinkled factotum, Croaknot, scurried to the monarch's side with impeccable subtlety. "Your Majesty, the travelling storyteller indicates his readiness to attend upon the court."

The king's eyes drifted, his lips pursing with sarcasm. "Most kind of him."

"Your Supreme Highness…" Croaknot bowed as far as his ancient bones would allow, his white hair flowing like seaweed in the tides beyond the castle cliff. He hurried away with flawless discretion.

There was a general clomping of footsteps and hissing of voices from the far end of the ballroom. Moments later, the ballroom's grand entrance opened to reveal a small man pulling a large cart. The queen snapped her fingers to gather the princes to her heel.

Croaknot adjusted the heavy chain of office wrapped around his shoulders. "Announcing licenced citizen Boneweed, certified of Episcopate 7," he called, as grandly as his ancient throat was able, "presenting himself to His Exulted Glory King Harlèd, the Conqueror, the Beneficent, the ninth

1

Vindicate, and to Her Royal Greatness Queen Ede, the Vilifier, and to their heirs, and to their court." He wheezed unobtrusively,.

Licenced citizen Boneweed was a short, thin man, with a head that was nearly spherical and topped with randomly swirled hair which clung valiantly to his scalp. His eyes were as dark as the night outside. His movements were languid, poised, almost as if his slender limbs defied gravity. His clothes had seen better days, long ago.

And so had his cart. It was twice his height and many times his width, and he heaved it along on a thick, coarse rope. It appeared to be no more than a huge wooden box on wheels, made of old planks and offcuts, held together with rusting strips of iron. Clustered on its rear surface were a series of pulleys and handles.

Its wheels squeaked like compressed mice as Boneweed manoeuvred the hefty cart so that it faced the royal gathering side-on. He delicately coiled the end of the rope on the floor and stepped forward, his emphatic smile unnerving rather than reassuring. The little princes huddled at the feet of their mother.

Boneweed gazed inquisitively at the king's magnificent whiskers, his glittering robes of state and the button nose for which his dynastic line was famous. He carefully considered the dour demeanour of the queen, her ruby lips, her towered hair and cross-strapped shoes.

"A thousand years to Your Majesty," he said. "A thousand years, My Queen," His voice was rasping but clear, a voice like ancient stone grinding down the empty millennia. "Herewith, I present my library."

He skipped to the rear of the cart, grasped the handle on a large metal wheel and turned it continuously in a quick, steady motion. With the clicking and ticking of inner cogs and ratchets, the top and bottom of the cart opened in intricate shapes, like a complex puzzle disentangling itself or a mouthful of jagged teeth widening for a bite.

Soft applause rose from the gloved hands of the courtiers seated behind the king and queen.

Inside the cart was a multi-layered festoon of boxes and shelves, drawers and compartments. Each enclosure was of a different design and every open surface was piled with thickly bound books or bundles of paper tied with ribbon or string.

"My library is of exotic and fearful heritage, dearest listeners—" While he spoke, Boneweed's spidery fingers plucked at a drawer and withdrew a small volume, no larger than his hand, and picked sharply through the roughly cut pages between its black, unmarked covers, "—for in it are gathered manuscripts from the seven corners of time itself, from worlds beyond our own, from places and centuries unknown to us. Some of these texts were summoned by nightmare arts, far off in the Oncetime, o so many backticks ago, when the land was new, when mystic energies wove truth from the stuff of dreams. Some came inverse-wise, from years yet to be. Some floated through the barriers at the Endovall, finding gaps in the waters wherein strange otherfolk peep at us. All tell of terrors, fears, warnings."

Queen Ede leaned closer to her husband. "Are you following this, Harlèd?"

"No," muttered the king. He placed his hands on the arms of his throne and raised his voice a little, as if speaking to a foreigner or a marshsquat. "Thank you, Citizen, a story, if you please."

Boneweed turned a page.

The Anxiety
Support Group

H'lo everyone, my name is Sam, and… Hi, yes. It's my first time at one of these meetings, so… Thank you, yes… Er, my problem is that… Oh, forgot, sorry. I…

Well, I have these three phobias. They're quite specific. I've had them for as long as I can remember, all my life, really, but they've got a lot worse in the last few years and they've, this is why I'm here, they've sort of combined recently, over about eighteen months or so. Sort of ganged up together, to kind of merge into one big phobia.

I've no idea why, I can't make sense of it. I haven't lost any loved ones, thank goodness. I have a happy marriage, a job that's not all that bad, most of the time, and we have enough to pay the bills. I'm very lucky, and very grateful that… I suppose I am drinking a bit more than I used to, although not that much, but that's because of the anxiety, not the other way around. I don't get drunk. My fears make me very upset and depressed, but I've avoided medication. I mean, it doesn't deal with the root issue, does it? And I want to understand *why*. I just don't know *why* I feel this way. I mean, my childhood wasn't filled with traumas, it was pretty standard as far as I can tell, and I've never been one of those people who likes danger or takes risks or anything like that. I don't understand why these thoughts… haunt me, I suppose. Plague me. It's got so bad, I… it's taking over my life…

Three phobias. The first one is a fear of, it sounds so stupid when I say it out loud, a terrible fear of irregular holes. It's actually got a name, it's called trypophobia. It's surprisingly common, actually. I get it when I see clusters of little holes which are different sizes. Just the word 'clusters' gives me the shudders. Like, the pock-marked skin on a toad's back, or clumps of bubbles on top of a frothy coffee, or sometimes corals or very seedy fruit. When I see these patterns I literally recoil, I flinch, I have to leave the room.

Regular patterns are usually fine. Polka dot dresses, the dimples on a gold ball, that sort of thing. Although honeycombs and shower heads can sometimes set me off. It's only where you get various sizes of circles or ovals grouped together. Fungal growths. Oily liquids.

I've read about it. Apparently, it's a psychological trigger linked to fears about things which are rotting or diseased.

I was first aware of this phobia when I was quite young. My aunt used to grow lotus flowers in her greenhouse, in a raised pond. The seed pods have an upper surface which can often… These horrible puckered holes with the actual seeds in them. I used to stare at the ugliest ones, transfixed, like an ophidiophobic watching a boa constrictor, or an aerophobic watching planes taxi. I'd get this sudden crawling sensation and I'd run away, shaking with fright.

My second phobia is of going blind. That's scotomaphobia. I suppose this one's a bit more understandable to most people. If you notice, these glasses I'm wearing have little transparent guard pieces on the sides, I can't bear the thought of grit or a bug or anything getting into my eyes. I'm actually quite relieved that I'm short-sighted enough to need glasses, otherwise I might be tempted to walk around in a pair of goggles.

The concept of, er… contact lenses makes me feel physically sick. Same goes if I see anyone with bloodshot eyes or a medical eye patch. I have a thorough check-up at the optician's every three months, and I'm never without a bottle of eye drops. There, see?

I expect this fear is an unhealthy consequence of my reading habits. I've always been a bookworm. Our house is like a library. I love books because they're such a personal thing, I mean, every story paints different pictures on the inside of your head, where only you can see them, don't you think?

If I lost my sight, I'd lose my mind. Never experiencing a printed page again... I'd panic. I'd lose all sense of reality, I couldn't live like that. Listening to someone reading aloud isn't the same thing, at all, and I know there's Braille, but all the visual joys of a book would be gone. Not having the simple comfort of looking at my bookshelves, being reminded of so many happy memories, would be unbearable. Worse than unbearable.

I can never sleep if it's pitch black. I'm not afraid of the darkness, I'm morbidly terrified that my eyesight might switch off and I wouldn't know.

My third phobia. It doesn't seem to have a name. Far too rare and particular, I suppose, but I don't see why. Encavmaphobia is a fear of being burned, but mine is the more precise fear of being cooked in an oven. Roasted alive. Yes, before you say anything, my early years were indeed self-policed for references to Hansel and Gretel. I remember being nine or ten and seeing a Tom and Jerry cartoon on TV, where a duckling gets put in a pot on a stove, and tied to a campfire spit, and slipped into one of those hefty 1940s-style cookers. It was the cooker that got me. The slam of the oven door. The click of the dial. I was so frightened I...

I've done the research, obviously. I'd fit into a modern oven, at least one of the larger catering models. I'm not very tall or very heavy, so in a foetal position... I've often wondered if this fear is just a form of claustrophobia, but other small spaces don't worry me much. And I can cope with using an oven to cook food in. As long as I can take my time and stay at an angle where I won't fall forward, and there's nobody behind me. Well, unless something's triggered a panic attack, such as being in a room where somebody says 'it's like an oven in here' in which case I can't set foot in the kitchen for at least a week. Good thing I'm a lousy cook, really.

The thing is, being roasted alive is *so* freakish and *so* ridiculously unlikely to happen, it ought to be the easiest phobia to deal with. But, of the three, it's become what you might call the dominant one.

Until now, I've never sought treatment for my fears, for the simple reason that I've learned to live with them. Or thought I had. They've been a pain in the backside, but not debilitating, as such, not life-ruining, so I've just worked around them, made adjustments, accomodated them. But now they've gradually merged into... I suppose I ought to call it a nightmare, except that it's not. I'm certain it's not.

I've had one or two recurring dreams over the years. I suppose we all have, haven't we? They were never fixed and identical. I used to have one which involved looking for a specific item in a shop that was going to close in a couple of minutes. Couldn't find it, clock ticking away. Each time I was searching for something different, or it was a different shop, or I was with different people, but it was always essentially the same dream.

This one, though. This nightmare. It's precisely the same every time, in every detail. It's driving me insane, it preys on my mind day and night. At first, it occurred about once a month, but it got more and more frequent until now it's every single night. Sometimes it seizes hold of me during the day, too, I terrified some poor kid on the bus the other week.

I come out of it screaming, I mean really screaming, and sometimes it takes hours for me to calm down and realise I'm safe. The only way I can get to sleep at all these days is through sheer exhaustion. When I'm awake I can't stop thinking about it, worrying about it. I can't concentrate, I can't rest. It's got to the point where life is becoming... very difficult.

I'm calling it a nightmare but, as I said, it's not. After you've had a bad dream, you know it was a dream no matter how real it seemed to you at the time. It might leave you disturbed or agitated, but you can appreciate that what you experienced was not the actual, three-dimensional, solid world. You might even interpret it as some sort of evil omen, or a twisted version of what's going on in your life, but when you wake up you *know* it wasn't a true, physical event, right? Well, this isn't like that. I can't tell the difference between the time I spend in the nightmare and the time I spend awake. They're equally... I don't know what you'd call it. Intense? Multi-sensory? It's like I'm actually living through something that's *happened*, over and over again in a loop. Only it *hasn't* happened, it's just my phobias!

Every time it's the same. *Exactly* the same. Sounds, objects, the order of events, everything, never any deviation in any way. It starts with...

I have a sensation of being pushed, hard. There are many hands shoving me along, I keep nearly tripping over my own feet. I'm hemmed in by these people, there must be a dozen of them or more, but I can't get a look at them because there's a hand pressing my head down and because my glasses have gone. I keep saying 'let me go' and 'why are you doing this?' but none of them answer me. I can hear their breathing and the scuffling of their feet. I'm frightened and confused, I don't know what's happening.

I'm pushed into a large room I've never seen before. Of course, I can't see properly without my glasses, but I get the impression that the building I'm in is as old as this one, although there are these light grey tiles on the floor and the first time the nightmare happened I wondered if I was in an office or a museum or something. Screwing up my eyes I can make out a few details and I realise I'm in a kitchen, and I'm wondering if this is a hotel, maybe, or a school or college, but I just can't tell.

And my heart is going like a steam engine, and I'm trembling with fear, and these people, this weird mob, start ripping my clothes away. And I get this sudden rush of panic when it finally dawns on me what they're going to do and that they're doing it for no reason at all. Just because they can. Just because the idea's been put into their heads.

I kick and scream, but they keep a tight hold on me. I'm pulling as hard as I can and I'm yelling for help but there's too many of them and, for every hand I manage to wriggle out of, another takes its place.

I hear the oven door clang open. My blood goes cold. I stop struggling for a moment because I'm fixed in terror on this big, black rectangle, surrounded by chrome, ahead of me. The oven has a drop-down opening, which forms a kind of shelf at about waist height. Someone pulls out a couple of metal grilles, to make room, and these grilles clatter to the tiles with a loud crash that makes me jump.

I'm shouting and pulling back. By now I've got nothing on and the floor is cold on my bare feet, and the air feels cold on my legs.

They're pushing me closer and closer and my eyes adjust the nearer I get and I can see the switches and timers over the top and the scrubbed black ridges inside. I can see it's electric rather than gas, and there's a round mesh at the back where the fan blows. I'm bucking and twisting like mad but I can't get free. I'm braying out these long howling wails, they're not even words any more.

They haul me up onto the door-stroke-shelf. It feels freezing cold on my skin at first and it creaks and rattles under my weight. They shove me inside rear-first, knees folded up to my chest, so my spine is against the mesh and my heels and scalp are scraping the sides.

The door is flung upwards, slammed shut. They must jam it somehow because no amount of slapping or hammering will budge it an inch. I can't break the big tinted glass panel but I can see out through it.

They're just standing there. Looking. I have both palms against the glass. It feels greasy. My screams are deafening in the confined space. I feel the inner surface touching me all over.

There are two loud clunks, of a knob being turned. Then a softer one, a button pressed. Instantly, the fan behind me switches on. A fresh burst of terror floods through me. I wail, I hit out frantically in any direction I can. The air becomes stifling. Hotter. All around. The sweat steams off me.

You might think this is when I wake up screaming, but it isn't. I don't wake until I die, and that's not for several minutes. The pain... searing pain... cuts into me... I... can't...

I said my phobias gang up. Where are the other two, you ask?

I watch my skin blister. Split. Pop. The fat beneath it liquifies. I become a repulsive, horrifying cluster of bubbling little holes.

And it's the last thing I see. Squeezed inside my skull, my eyes boil. I am blind. And alive for a few seconds yet.

I... sorry, I... it's kind of you all to not look disgusted... I'm trapped in this unchanging, repeating vision. Maybe that's the word I want, 'vision'? Whatever it is, I've had all I can stand.

I keep six fans going full blast by my bed at night. I keep the bath filled with cold water. Nothing helps. My throat's permanently sore from the screaming when I wake up. I can't take it any more.

I wasn't sure about coming here tonight, but... Thank you for listening, it does feel better to, you know, talk. I'm grateful for the chance to tell you all about it. Thank you...

Oh, is the session over? I mean, if everyone's standing up?... Ah, this isn't one of those group hug things, is it? I'm really not a hugger, I'm afraid. Oh! Er, excuse me, those are my glasses. Could I have them back, please, I...

No, wait a minute. No, please, let me go. Why are you doing this? Let me go. Let me go! Let me go! Where are you taking me? Let me go! Let! Me! Go!

Boneweed bowed to each throne in turn as he gently closed the book and set it aside. The king and queen glanced at each other. The servants and courtiers glanced at the king and queen.

Queen Ede leaned closer to her husband. "Did you understand any of that, Harlèd?"

"Not a word," muttered the king. "Perhaps it is progressive?" The evening's banquet lay heavily on his stomach and he was sure he could feel gas forming in pockets throughout his innards. He gave Boneweed the smile he used when addressing crowds in the Lower Courtyard. "These are of your own composition, Citizen?"

"No, Your Majesty," said Boneweed, fluttering over the books and papers, "I am but their custodian and curator. Their assembling has been my lifetime's dedicated labour. No other library in existence stirs the dark bewitchments to which—"

The king paddled his hand. "You may continue, Citizen."

Regime Change
part 1: the interview

The Goat And Hen, being full of snug little cubicles and old oak partitions, was an ideal pub for quiet meetings. Apart from the area beside the bar, where the regulars thumped opinions and threw darts, the atmosphere of the place was subdued and discreet. Every night of the week, the off-white walls and the worn seating heard a blackmailer's dream of confessions, transactions, liaisons.

On a chilly evening in November, Terry Nixon, author of true crime paperbacks such as *The UK's Greatest Murderers Volume 3* and *The Eye-Socket Press Book Of Serial Killers*, nestled uncomfortably into one of the two monk's benches which formed the sides of a booth near the entrance. The edge of the screwed-down table squished the dome of his stomach and he took the third sip of his pint since he'd left the bar. The glass was cold and wet in his hand. He dotted the base of it two, three times along the table's sticky surface, leaving linked rings of moisture.

He'd drunk most of his lager by the time DC Stokes arrived a minute or so later. Despite the police officer's plain clothes, the flashing neon sign that said 'copper,' the one his job kept fixed on the top of his head, was bright enough to set the regulars looking in the other direction. He scouted around for a moment or two, spotted Nixon and hurriedly swerved himself onto the other bench. To Nixon, young Stokes was a leather jacket and haircut, a cleanly shaved chin and his girlfriend's preferred aftershave. To Stokes, middle aged Nixon was an unwashed shirt and the smell of vapes.

"Don't you want a drink?" said Nixon, nodding at the bar.

"No," said Stokes, shaking his head. Nervous impatience kept twitching his face. When Nixon took a Tascam recorder from his anorak pocket, Stokes waved it away. "I don't want any record of this. And no blog, vlog, podcast, nothing. Sorry."

"Eh?" grimaced Nixon. "What, suddenly you don't trust--?"

"No record. At all. Not on this. Sorry. I know it sounds paranoid but there's good reason." He paused for a moment, glancing at the bar. "I wasn't even going to sit down. I was going to type it all out, print it, delete the file, come in here, give it you and walk out. Then I remembered printers can be traced."

"Delete the file?" frowned Nixon with a half-laugh. He leaned over the table, pressing his stomach into a letter B. "Have you stumbled onto something MI5-y?"

Stokes ran a frustrated hand through his haircut. "No, no. For fuck's sake. Nothing like that."

"But isn't that why you put the note through my door?"

"I'm not tech savvy enough to dodge all the algorithms, I didn't want to use email or anything. You never know what system's reading it these days, do you? Look, I'm sorry, of course I know I can trust you, you know that, but…"

Nixon, sensing a wasted journey, felt the need to administer a little professional reassurance. "I never let your old dad down on that score, did I? And I've never let you down. Sources are sacred." He also felt the need for another pint. "You sure you don't want a drink? You look like you need one."

"No," said Stokes. He was still for a second or two. "I'm thinking of leaving the job. Dad was a natural at it. I'm not. I think I only joined up so he wouldn't give me that disappointed look."

Nixon felt a sharp pang of irritation that, on top of a wasted journey, a valuable contact might be lost to him. "Does Hannah know?"

"I haven't said anything to her," said Stokes quietly. "I haven't told her about what I'm here to tell you, either. I don't know what might happen."

"You couldn't get me that interview transcript, then?" said Nixon. "Since there's no plain brown envelope for me?"

"This is not like other times," said Stokes. There was a snag of emotion in his voice that Nixon had never heard before. "There'd be consequences, guaranteed."

"But you *were* at the crime scene you mentioned?"

"Yes," said Stokes with a hint of impatience. "I got there about an hour after the suspect was arrested."

The crime scene was one of a cluster of old, detached cottages on the west side of the village. All were much the same, two storey homes with a small kitchen extension jutting out either at the side or the back. By the time Stokes arrived, the crime scene's front garden had been churned to mud with back-and-forth activity.

After the previous night's heavy rain there was a steady dripping from the cracked guttering in the eaves. A front window on the ground floor had been opened, to help clear the metallic, cesspit stink inside. The forensics team were still keeping numbers in the house to a minimum, so Stokes was assigned to questioning neighbours. No, didn't hear nothing, yes, very nice people, never any trouble, can't believe it, always the quiet ones.

Stokes pinched at his nose every time he walked past the cottage and caught the scent. Through the open window he glimpsed furniture piled up, stains on the wallpaper.

Half a dozen residents from the other side of the village just happened to accidentally on purpose walk their dogs along the perimeter of the Do Not Cross tape. The dogs were either snarling and straining at the leash, or else cowering behind their owner's legs. To clear the area at maximum speed, Stokes asked the villagers if anyone would like to make a statement.

There were other rubberneckers in sight, a dozen or more of them, dotted all around the cottage in groups of two or three, watching from half a field's distance. Because they remained still and silent, and kept well back, nobody at the crime scene bothered to chase them off. Stokes thought there was something creepy about them, about the way none of them spoke or pointed. They'd disappeared within an hour or two.

"The bodies weren't moved 'till later in the day," said Stokes. "I didn't see any of that."

"There were three of them, right?" said Nixon.

Stokes nodded. "Next day it was pure chance I was at the suspect's questioning. We were short of staff."

"Who's the lead?"

"Ray Gowan. I think you've met him, yes? Big bloke, that's right. They put Walker in Interview Room 3. You probably know, that's the one closest to help, they use it for interviewing suspects in violent cases. Which I never understood, because the ones that kick off are always the low-level sort who haven't the sense to realise they're beaten. But Walker scared the hell out of me, right from the second we entered the room. I'd been told he was covered in blood from scalp to toe when he was brought in. None of it his own, except for where he's cut off his own privates. His hands and arms were bandaged because he'd been tearing at them in his cell, bleeding onto the floor and using it as ink to draw shapes on the walls."

Walker was a slackly skinned man in his fifties, wet-lipped, with a flat nose and a rambling comb-over. He was pale and greasy-looking, and what appeared to be a dark patch of eczema showed behind the collar of his police-issue shirt. He'd been thoroughly cleaned up, then dosed up to keep him calm.

Interview Room 3 was the most sparse in the building, with sky blue flooring and walls plain enough to make a coroner's office look vibrant and inviting. A battered wooden table and chairs, official audio recording gear and a panic strip circling the room at mid-height were all it contained.

That day's duty solicitor, perching next to Walker in a fug of his own indifference, was a weaselly, corpse-thin bastard called Harcourt. He shifted and sniffed, pointing to where he required Walker to sign here, here, and here, then sifting through the sheets of notes in front of him.

Walker sat with his upper body making tiny circular movements from the hip, but it was his eyes which unnerved Stokes the most. They were perfectly symmetrical, inverted semi-circles which almost seemed fake until he blinked. He looked at Stokes and Ray Gowan sitting opposite him, his gaze steady and penetrating, his mouth set in a crooked smile like a crocodile's.

The two police officers had notebooks and pens at the ready, and Stokes switched on the audio recorder. Gowan looked down at his hastily scribbled interview plan, then launched into the standard preamble, his words rapid and automatic, spoken in a near-monotone. He stated the date, location and suspect's details, followed by "I am Detective Sergeant Ray Gowan, Avon and Somerset Police, also present are..."

"Detective Constable Steven Stokes," he said, his mouth suddenly dry.

"Simon Harcourt acting as legal representative for the defendant."

"Jeffrey Alan Walker," said DS Gowan, "you are here because you have been arrested for the suspected murders of Elizabeth Mary Walker aged fifty-five years, Henry Leonard Jones aged forty-seven years and Sarah Emilia Walker aged forty-nine years, contrary to common law... Do you understand these charges?"

"Yes. Yes, yes," smiled Walker, nodding. His voice was deep and he spoke with a slight, indeterminate accent.

Gowan's quick, flat tone told Stokes that his colleague's thoughts were a long way ahead of his words. "During this interview I will ask you about the circumstances relating to these charges and about events which took place at 13 Meadow Lane, Hernbridge, last night. I will also ask you about anything else which may arise in order to properly establish the facts pertaining to these events. You are encouraged to voice any issue you feel is relevant and to consider carefully your answers before giving them. You have a right to silence. Whatever you say may be used against you in a court of law. During the course of this interview you do not have to say anything but it may harm your defence if you do not mention something when questioned which you later rely on in court. Everything you say will be recorded and may be played to a court if you plead not guilty to the charges and there is a subsequent trial. Your legal representative has been given notice of how to obtain a copy of this interview in accordance with the Police And Criminal Evidence Act, Code E, paragraph 4.19. The interview has no time limit and you may request a break at any point. Both myself and my colleague will be present throughout the interview and either of us may ask you questions and write notes... Do you understand the purpose of this interview and your right to silence as I have just outlined them?"

Walker nodded cheerfully.

"For the benefit of the recording, the suspect has nodded," said Gowan. He sat back for a moment, gathering his thoughts and flicking glances at his notes. "OK, Jeffrey, I'd like you to tell us what happened last night."

The solicitor placed a hand on the table, side-on and precise, like a suspended karate chop. "Owing to the seriousness of the allegations against him, I've advised my client to answer no comment to all questions."

"They came!" squealed Walker, so loudly and eagerly that the other three men all jumped. "They came!"

"Who did?" said Gowan.

"Mr Walker, I've told you--" began the solicitor.

Walker chuckled. "The little people! Little, little people... The shadows... Up they crawled, one by one, then faster and faster, scampering. I don't know how many. Lots. Lots."

"I don't understand what you mean by 'little people,' Jeffrey," said Gowan. "Do you mean children?"

"No!" scoffed Walker. "I mean the heralds, bringing the good news. The reeking fiends, the demons, the hag-imps and the hob-spirits. We heard their agonies and their scuttling feet. We felt their cold claws all over our skin."

"Demons," said Gowan flatly. "Crawling up from... what, Hell, presumably?"

"We called them," cried Walker, as if he was recalling a win on the lottery, "and they answered."

The solicitor sat up awkwardly. "I'd like time to consult my client about--"

"Nothing in his medical history," said Gowan firmly, keeping his eyes on Walker. "We already looked. Nothing chemical in his system, anywhere, OK? He hasn't even been to his GP in years."

DC Stokes cleared his throat. "Mr, er, Jeffrey, how exactly did you call them?"

Walker's attention switched to Stokes and the young detective felt himself shudder. Walker's eyes burned with an inner fire, not of anger or insanity but of joy. He was excited and happy, like a kid who knows exactly what's under the wrapping on his birthday present before he tears it open. An echo of the crime scene's smell tickled Stokes's nose and he swatted nervously at his nostrils.

Walker was delighted to answer the question. "We followed the instructions we'd been given," he grinned. "First, I took the knife, the very sharpest I could find, and—"

"Instructions from whom?" said Gowan. "From where?"

"From our Lord," said Walker quietly, humbly. "We follow His word. I took the knife, and I slit the belly. He screamed and screamed."

"He?" said Gowan.

"Henry, my friend Henry," said Walker.

"Henry Leonard Jones," said Gowan.

The solicitor suddenly snapped his fingers and pointed to the audio recorder until Stokes pressed Pause. "This mad sod," he said, slowly and wearily, without looking at his client, "needs either a man in a white coat or a fucking priest. Why hasn't he had a proper evaluation?"

"With offences like--" began Gowan.

The solicitor's gaze fixed on the table ahead of him. "Mr Walker, I strongly advise you--"

Walker pawed at him with one bandaged hand. "Don't go, don't go, listen to the good news!"

"Get off me!" spat the solicitor.

Stokes took his finger off the Pause button. "Jeffrey," said Gowan in a commanding tone, trying to regain Walker's attention, "would you clarify that for me, please? Where was Henry when this happened?"

Walker almost tripped over his own words in his eagerness to tell them. "In the front room, we were all in the front room, all four of us, ready skyclad. We waited for the proper time, like the instructions written in our heads said, and I had the honour to say the first words, loud and clear. Henry stood up, Lizzie held him by one arm and Sarah by the other. Henry watched the clock on the wall behind me, the big one Lizzie and me got from B&M, and when it was time he said now, then I slit him. And it went all over me! All over the carpet! Henry was shaking and screaming but he didn't fall, bless him. Lizzie and Sarah caught loads of it in plastic boxes from the kitchen. They were laughing, I was laughing. Henry's guts were starting to come out. I said the next words and I dipped my fingers in one of the boxes and I started on the writing. Lizzie and Sarah helped, they did most of it, actually, as far up the walls as they could reach, I did the bits above because I'm taller. I cut off Henry's nose, and his eyelids, and his lips, and I put them in the correct places while I carried on with the words. The ladies were, like, me too, me too, so when I got to the right place I opened them with my knife down and across like the picture in the instructions. Henry was on his back now and I cut some flesh from his bones and laid it out carefully. They were all still alive when the first demons appeared, I was really happy they got to see that. And so many arrived! I took the knife and I sliced off what I was told. The demons smiled while I ate it, then everything was complete. They are here now. Forever. Forever and ever, Amen. I don't remember what happened next, I was sitting on the carpet for a long while. I saw the lights of the police cars through the curtains."

Walker stopped speaking as abruptly as he'd started. The solicitor sat beside him looking stony-faced and sweaty. For a moment, the only sound in the interview room was the soft murmur of voices and activity that filtered in from the busy area outside.

From beneath his notes, Gowan slid three A4 photos, each showing a different sheet of paper crammed from edge to edge with tiny, intricate symbols. He spun them with two fingers and pushed them across the table to make a line in front of Walker. "For the benefit of the tape, I am showing the suspect three photographs taken at 13 Meadow Lane, Hernbridge, reference 618-a to 618-c. Jeffrey, what can you tell me about what's shown in these photographs?"

Walker beamed. "For months, many months, they've been telling me what will happen, so I wrote it all down. Lots to remember. They whispered to me, from where they were, on the other side of the Great Veil—"

"The demons?"

"Yes, they told me about His plans, to claim the world as His own, at last, to control it entirely, to renew it. It was all so very exciting. I didn't listen properly, at first. I thought I might be making a mistake, or confusing the true meaning of what I was being told. But as soon as I gave myself up to Him I started to understand."

"Did they speak to Lizzie too?" said Stokes, making an effort to steady the tremble in his voice. "And Henry? And Sarah?"

"Yes," said Walker. "Eventually. The whispering came from very far away, so you had to really listen hard. The others were really pleased when they heard it too. The whispering told me how to summon the little people, what I had to do and say, and I wrote it down. So we did exactly what they said and they came! They're gathering, on the Earth, preparing us, preparing for the new world. They've come to watch the fun. It's nearly time."

"Time for what?" I said.

"The wild hunt," said Walker. "The great celebration of death, when the faithful and the chosen shall rise up as one and dance in blood. And all the world shall be changed in His image. Very soon, His kingdom is come!"

With a sudden cry of alarm, the solicitor jumped to his feet, looking down at Walker. "Oh shit!" He stepped back, noisily knocking over his chair.

Walker's expression flipped to one of amused guilt, a toddler found with his hands in the biscuit tin. He stood up too and as he did so he plucked something out of his upper leg. He'd been digging with the solicitor's pen since the start of the interview, and one side of his trousers was soaked red. A gout of blood popped out along with the nib.

Gowan slapped the panic strip that ran along the wall and the alarm sounded outside.

Walker skipped back to avoid Stokes grabbing hold of him. Gowan swerved around the table but before either of them could get any closer Walker had launched himself on top of the solicitor, pulling him to the floor, stabbing at his eyes. The man's screams was deafening in such a small room.

Shouts and heavy footsteps approached the door. Gowan seized Walker by his shoulders and hauled him aside. Walker twisted around and punched Gowan so hard on the nose that the detective jerked backwards violently, knocking over both Stokes and the table.

Stokes was visibly shaky. "You're going to have to take my word for what happened next. I'm not a suggestible or a very imaginative person. I certainly don't believe in possession and all that shite."

Nixon's chubby fingers fumbled at his empty beer glass. Stokes paused for a moment, a mixture of worries scattered over his face. "I honestly can't explain this, but I know what I saw. I promise you, I *promise* you, I am not exaggerating. Walker was on his feet. There were other officers trying to get in, shouting, but the door kept hitting the table where it had fallen over. Ray Gowan had backed into me and we were both on the floor. Ray had his hands clapped to his face, I couldn't reach Walker. The solicitor kept up this bloody awful high-pitched scream. And... the room got darker. I *swear* to you. The overhead light did not dim, I could see it clearly from where I was, the room suddenly got darker and icy cold. I saw Walker's breath suddenly misting in front of his face. He looked up, and he was grinning. And above all the other noise, I heard him call out. I'm here, he said. I'm here."

"Is this when he killed himself?" muttered Nixon.

"He didn't kill himself," said Stokes, with a sudden intensity that made Nixon blanch. He shook his head, his hands propping up his temples. "In the report, I had to say it was all down to him. What else *could* I say?"

He looked up, his face filled with a lingering terror which even a practised old cynic like Nixon could see was already a burden, a heavy and lifelong weight on the young man's peace of mind. "There was a shadow, in the corner," said Stokes, "where there hadn't been one before. There was nothing in the room that could have made it. Nothing! It was just *there*. A shape… horrible… twisted and horrible…"

"How many saw it?"

"Ray Gowan saw it too, I know. The desk sergeant was half way through the door by now, he must have seen it. One or two others, maybe. It was behind Walker, kind of crouching over him. He must have seen the shock on my face, because he spun around to look at it. Then he turned back, grinning all over his face. This only took a second. He was all, like, there you are, told you so. He bent over, lowered his head. He didn't jump, or throw himself, as I put in the report. The shadow, it kind of… bloomed… and vanished in the same instant Walker shot across the room head first. This force of movement just seemed to burst through the air. You know what the lab said? They said he hit the wall at close to 300psi. That's harder than being hit by a fucking lorry! I was still shaking hours later, when I typed everything up. Couldn't keep my fingers still. Ray Gowan was at A&E with a broken nose. They managed to save the sight in one of the solicitor's eyes… They got rid of the stains and repaired the wall but nobody likes to use that interview room any more. And it's stayed freezing cold in there, too, no matter what you do."

"Ideal for getting quick confessions?" said Nixon. He regretted the words the moment they passed his lips, but Stokes seemed to ignore them.

"What Walker said, about the little people, and seeing that shadow, it got to me. Hannah kept asking what was wrong, but I couldn't tell her. When you asked about the investigation, I was almost relieved to have an excuse to go over it. Face up to it, you know. But…"

Stokes leaned in, his voice dropping to a whisper. "This is why I wanted to meet like this, why I didn't want to email. Yes, I'm feeling bloody paranoid and it's nothing to do with Walker, or what he did. Nothing at all. I already had a list of the relevant files on the system, including the crime scene photos. When I looked again, on all of them, every button on the screen was greyed out. Couldn't open them, print them, nothing. Restricted access is nothing new, as you well know, but this was evidence I'd logged, in an active investigation. I thought it must be a mistake. Ray Gowan was back at work so I left my desk and went to check with him, but *in the corridor* our new DCI, Greg Halsey – he was with the Met, I don't think you'd know him? – he stopped me and asked me why I'd tried to access those files. This wasn't even two minutes afterwards! Those files were tagged. And not just tagged, but tagged for intervention by a senior officer. I was shaking like a leaf. Halsey's a very tall bloke, and he stands in your personal space at the best of times, so there I was, a bag of nerves, smelling his cheese and onion crisps, trying to tell him that all I was doing was reviewing the case. And he said to me, this is word for word, he said to me Steven the Jeffrey Walker case is closed and is none of your business, is that clear? I was taken aback for a minute, and I said something about needing to check something with Ray Gowan. And

Halsey said… He said it in a tone as nice as pie, but every word felt like he was breaking bones with a pair of pliers. He said, you will not discuss the case with anyone, either inside this nick or outside this nick. If you so much as grunt the name Jeffrey Walker in your sleep, you will face criminal charges so vile even your own mother will disown you, do you understand me?"

"He *said* that?" whispered Nixon.

Stokes nodded. "In those precise words, I swear to you. When I happened to see Ray Gowan, a couple of hours later, the look on his face told me he'd had *exactly* the same bollocking. He said nothing. I said nothing. Since then, we've compared notes well out of earshot, but there's no proof of anything. I tell you, Terry, I am angry and I am scared. I can't shake it. I don't know what the fuck is going on, but *something* is going on."

"The interview tape's gone, I assume? Along with any CCTV?"

"Of course."

Nixon felt a dryness in his throat which had nothing to do with his lack of another pint. "Might be worth trying the lawyer. Simon Harcourt, was it?"

"I was never here," whispered Stokes, jittery and guarded like an unburdened penitent whose relief is suddenly outweighed by the rawness of disclosure. "You got none of this from me, OK?"

"OK."

Stokes slunk away, surreptitiously enough not to disturb the regulars at the bar. After he'd gone, one of them – bearded, anonymous – turned to stare blankly at Nixon, who sat pondering for a minute or two, palms rubbing at his stubbled chin, thoughts rolling in time with his stomach. The anonymous man kept surreptitiously watching him.

The journalist took his glass to the bar and got a refill, perching on a tall bar stool like a lollipop on a stick. He didn't doubt Stokes's sincerity, not for a moment. The lad simply didn't have the turn of mind it took to make up a story like that. But there had to have been some kind of misinterpretation, somewhere along the line. I mean, murders like that, perpetrated by a man so obviously deranged. The horrible creepiness of it all was bound to affect anyone's judgement. Obviously. Didn't make sense, otherwise. Hmm, see what the lawyer said. Whichever way it went, in the end, it would make a good chapter in the next paperback.

With a grunt, Nixon heaved himself down, the toes of his scuffed trainers pointing to meet the floor, and straightened his coat. He suddenly noticed the anonymous regular who was still watching him, silent and unmoving. For a split second Nixon felt a flutter of anxiety.

Huh, just jittery over Stokes' stories, probably. Or indigestion. Snorting to himself with amusement, he made his way towards the door. The anonymous man tracked his movement then got up and, without a word to his companions and without them asking him where he was going, he followed Nixon out onto the street.

runting, King Harlèd shifted forward a little, his joints feeling slightly stiff. "Citizen Boneweed," he smiled humourlessly, "we are aware that the night is dark, that your cart is heavy, and that the road up the mountainside is long. I would advise, then, to make your efforts worthwhile. Where are the kings and queens in your narratives? Where are the bold swordsweepers and the wise officials?"

Boneweed blinked his big black eyes. Flickery light, from the ballroom's warming braziers, danced in yellow across his strange wooden cart.

"I regret, Your Majesty," he rasped, "no story that is in my possession concerns the actions of either a king or a queen."

There was silence throughout the room for a moment, then the king guffawed so heartily that fragments of the evening's banquet hopped out from between his teeth and littered his knees and whiskers. "Come now, Citizen, a story is without worth or meaning if it doesn't feature the listener. Is that not the iron ruling of the Academie?"

Boneweed shrugged. "Perhaps so, Your Majesty, but the Academie has also ruled that I am ineligible for its membership and thus I am unbound by its prohibitions."

A ripple of contained disgust circled the courtiers. For a moment, King Harlèd puzzled over the meaning of the traveller's words, while Croaknot the factotum drifted prudently to his side.

"Your Infinite Sagacity," he wheezed, shifting his weighty chain of office, "you may remember Adjustment 395 of last mooncycle's Council? By your gracious consent the Academie was replaced as Sole Arbiter..." He paused, choosing his words with precision, hoping that the king would recall the solution found to the problem of the monarch's third concubine's singing career. "...In the interests of including a broader representation of artistic—"

"Yes, of course," said the king, with a yes-of-course nod. "Proceed, Citizen Boneweed."

Croaknot, to save wear and tear on his ancient knees, decided to stay put at the king's side. Queen Ede, by finger and eye, ordered the braziers stoked to keep out the night's chill.

Boneweed slid a tall volume from a compartment on his cart. "As you listen, so the weave of my library's sorcery shall en-web the hearts of all." The slyness in his voice, and the peculiar leer that danced upon his odd face, put a knot of uneasiness in the queen's stomach. The little princes, sensing disturbance, clung tightly to their mother's legs.

It's Been A Lovely Day

At shortly after 8 a.m., Mrs Harris opened her front door and began to ferry fold-up garden chairs out to the big circular area of grass she always called the village green. She called it the village green even though Hillside Drive wasn't in a village and, after a week or more of hot and sunny days, the grass was more a bleachy straw colour than green.

Numbers 67 to 83 were set well back from the road, forming a kind of staggered U-shape on their own. The green was in the middle of the U and was mown by workmen from the District Council every third Wednesday of the month between April and October.

Mrs Harris drew a long, slow lungful of clear morning air. The last of the night's coolness was fading lazily into the strengthening sunshine, and someone not far away was cooking breakfast. She shut her eyes and felt the warmth on her face, the gentle breeze in her hair.

She looked up. Above the village green, at a slowly varying angle above the horizon, an amorphous shape spun in the blue sky, illuminated on one side by the sun. At 8:27am, from ground level, it still looked only half the size of the Moon.

The Harrises at No.75 had eight garden chairs in their shed, although they almost never used more than three of them at a time. Mrs Harris set out the four newer ones, the ones with the cup holders in the arm rests, at the edge of the green and put the four older ones, in the floral pattern, two to each side.

Mr Jenkins and his picnic table emerged from No.71. Both of them were knackered with age, their edges tattered, their joints creaky, but they wore their vintage with a certain pride, Mr Jenkins in collar and tie, the table with its original Formica surface. "Do we want any more, d'you think?" he puffed, clicking legs open beside the chairs. "I could fetch me coffee table?"

"No, I'm sure this'll be fine, Cyril," said Mrs Harris brightly. "We'll just put out all the food and drinks and everyone can help themselves. Here, would you like a seat?"

"Actually," he said, patting at the belly of his tank top, "I thought I might bring me armchair out. If one of your lads would kindly give me a hand?"

"Good idea," said Mrs Harris. She called back into the house. "Josh! Job for you!"

Mr Jenkins squinted upwards. "Going to be a warm one again."

"Yes," sighed Mrs Harris. "The forecast said high twenties." She sniffed a little, a smile flashing her face, and she swatted at a stray fly on the skirt of her Special Occasion dress.

Josh Harris, heavy with teenage schlump, followed Mr Jenkins back into No.71. His brother Michael lolled out of his bedroom window, taking in the scene on the green then tilting his chin up and watching the deep, even pink glowing through closed eyelids.

The Pimlotts, next door to the Harrises, emerged like a sports team jogging out onto the playing field, all of them in fancy dress. The three little girls each wore their party princess outfits – pink, blue, blue – complete with tiaras. The youngest waved her home-made magic wand, topped with a glitter-shedding cardboard star that waggled on sticky tape. Their parents were a tiger and a pirate.

Mrs Harris stretched her eyes and applauded. "Girls, you look so beautiful!" She cocked her head at the youngest. "Are you going to cast us a few spells, Daisy?"

Daisy scrunched her face for a moment then nodded vigorously. Her sisters stood spinning at the hip.

"Ahoy there, me hearties," said their mum, doing the voice quite well, "these scurvy knaves were going to stay in their jim-jams all day, until me n' Cap'n Tiger said we'd join in."

"Captain Tiger's already feeling a bit hot in this," said Mr Pimlott, tugging at the stripey collar of his costume. "Do you like our badges?" All five of them thrust out their chests, on which were pinned cardboard discs declaring We're The Pimlotts.

"There's team spirit!" laughed Mrs Harris. In the momentary silence which followed, she exchanged wistful looks with Mrs Pimlott.

Josh staggered back onto the village green with Mr Jenkins's armchair balanced upside down, the seat against the top of his head, his hands gripped onto the chair's soft arms. "Where d'you want it?" he grunted unsteadily.

"Next to the others, there, please," said Mr Jenkins, a cushion tucked under each arm. "Thank you very much, young man, thank you."

Josh nodded, his face beetroot with exertion. "That thing's bloody heavy," he muttered as he passed his mum. Mrs Harris, proud of her boy, watched his sloping shoulders lollop into the house to fetch plates, cutlery and his brother.

It wasn't long before the other residents of the semi-circle were out enjoying the morning sunshine too. Pimlotts, Burtons, Greenes, Hamiltons, Abbots, Willises and more. Even the starchy old woman who lived at the end house, and who only ever communicated with the outside world via frowns, sniffs and curt notes shoved through letterboxes, brought a foldable work table out onto her front path and sat doing a jigsaw.

The residents ate bacon rolls and drank coffee. They chatted about this and that, or one thing and another. From about 9:30 a.m. Mr Pimlott and Mr Greene, as they'd promised the previous week, organised games for everyone. Some picnic blankets were spread out – tartan, stripy, plain – overlapping each other to create an area for board games. Cricket stumps marked the goals for mini-football using a tennis ball. A leftover can of spray paint made lines at the roadside end of the grass, for running races.

The younger residents wanted to have a go at everything. The older ones each picked out two or three games to play and the rest of the time formed a whistling, cheering band of spectators. Mr Hamilton's posh chess set from Hong Kong was much admired, there was a tense play-off for dominoes champion, and both the Hundred Yards Running Backwards and the Sprint With A Bucket On Your Head events had to be re-started because half the contestants couldn't stop either laughing or cheating. The children became quite competitive, but not nearly as competitive as the dads, who were nowhere near as competitive as the mums.

At 11:45 a.m., one person from each household went indoors to switch on various ovens, hobs and air fryers. Most of the food for the communal lunch had been prepared a day or two ago and only needed reheating.

Soon, while the Blindfolded Bowls tournament was finishing and the smaller kids were having a last impromptu jumping race, delicious smells began to waft across the village green.

Mrs Harris stepped carefully, gripping a huge oval plate on which steamed an entire golden roasted turkey. "Where did you get that?" gasped Mrs Pimlott.

"Forward planning," grinned Mrs Harris. "I've had this hidden in the freezer since March."

Mrs Greene appeared with an enormous, teetering dish of various meaty and fishy nibbles in breadcrumbs, Mr Willis brought out potatoes done three different ways, and Mr Hamilton contributed a big pan of his famous vegetable stew. Out came heirloomed crockery and gravy boats, bowls of steamed peas and carrots, white tablecloths carried over forearms and shoulders. There were fizzy drinks for the kids and beers, wines and every spirit imaginable for the grown-ups.

All the residents gathered for lunch. The original idea had been to put all the tables in a long line, street party style, but it seemed nicer to form them into one big square, so the different dishes could be passed around without hassle and to make it easier for people to join in conversations.

The hum and gaggle of voices was punctuated by the fssssh of cans, the pop of corks, the glug of liquids into the Willis' expensive crystal glassware. The teenagers were allowed *one* can of beer or *one* glass of wine and *maybe* another one later on, OK? The background clatter of knives and forks was like the tinkling of a dozen wind chimes or the chittering of tiny metal birds.

Mrs Harris pushed her fold-out chair back a little and walked over to the starchy old woman at the end house. They spoke for a minute or more, Mrs Harris with head cocked over the starchy old woman's half-finished jigsaw and the starchy old woman looking up and down, from neighbour to Alpine Scene and back again, her bony fingers turning a piece of sky over and over. Then both of them walked back to the table, the old woman carrying her chair. Some shuffling and a spare plate later she was in between Mr Burton and the youngest of the Pimlott sisters. She was welcomed with raised glasses and returned the greeting with a series of smiling nods while she pocketed her piece of sky and poked at the tablecloth. She ate two helpings of turkey, roasties and veg, drank almost half a bottle of brandy, and was soon flat out on the grass, spread-eagled and snoring.

At 1:30pm the residents reckoned they could juuuuust about squeeze in a bit of pudding, so they all had cake, or ice cream, or cake with ice cream on top. After that, the dinner table was left to its own devices, with plates scattered wherever and the remaining food – of which there wasn't much – put into plastic tubs in case anyone felt peckish later on.

Some dragged their chairs into little enclaves, to chat. Some lay out on the grass, in the sunshine. The children chased each other around, squealing, or fetched toys from their rooms and made a miniature town from dolls' houses, model cars and action figures. Glasses were refilled and an atmosphere of gentle bonhomie settled on the village green like a soft blanket.

Mrs Harris sat with Mr and Mrs Pimlott, the Greenes and Mr Jenkins. She kicked off her shoes and stretched her toes on the ground, feeling every blade of the dry grass and the dusty surface of the earth.

She could almost sense the life beneath her feet, in the soil, the earthworms, the tiny insects, the plant seeds, the billion microscopic things that made their home down there in the dark. All in the web of nature, herself included. She felt at peace, with the warm sunlight on her feet and the trill of sparrows in the trees.

It was 2:25pm. Chat turned to reminiscences about family and friends. Mrs Pimlott, still dressed as a pirate but now minus the plastic cutlass and the eye patch, had everyone in stitches with stories about her accident-prone great-aunt. "She was just one of those people, you know, every time you saw her she'd either fallen down a hole or accidentally given away her shoes or *something*. She drove a brand new car into the sea at Swanage once."

"What?" spluttered Mrs Harris.

"Yup. She's tootling along, thinks ah at last, there's a parking space. But it's not, it's a fishing jetty, and she's driving straight ahead and wondering why all these anglers are shouting at her. How rude! And then, whop, off the end, into the sea.

"Was she OK?" laughed Mr Greene.

"Not a scratch, for once, but the rescue crew who turned up were laughing so much they couldn't winch the car out for half an hour. She was fuming."

Mr Greene told them about the time he'd turned up to the wrong job interview, and about some of the practical jokes he and his friends had played on each other at university. Laughter rolled across the village green, drinks clinked, and some of the other adults sat on the grass to keep an eye on the children and talk about their travels to interesting places around the world and the impressive sights they'd seen.

Mr Jenkins sat with his arms around a dusty old photo album. His story, about his very first arrest as a copper, got the longest, loudest laugh of all.

"I didn't know you were in the police," said Mrs Harris.

"This were donkey's years ago," said Mr Jenkins. "My Angela made me give it up the day I come home with two black eyes and a stab wound. That's when I got the shop. Anyway, I were just out of Hendon, first month on the job, and I were on foot patrol at night, around the town. And about three in the morning I heard this alarm go off on the high street, so I legged it over there and this jeweller's place had been broken into, smash and grab. And the owner lived in the flat above, he said this is terrible, what am I going to to? So I said to him, leave it with me, sir, I said. Twenty minutes later, about half a mile away, I knocked on this fella's door. What d'you want? he said. I said, I am arresting you for the theft of jewels from the high street. And he looked completely thunderstruck, and then he sort of slumped and said a'right, a'right, I did it. How the 'ell did you know it were me? I made sure there were no fingerprints, no witnesses, nothing. And here you are! I take my hat off to you, Constable, I really do, that's unmatched detective work, I tell you. How *the hell* did you know it were me? And I raised a finger, and then I pointed it straight down, at the three foot of snow on the ground, and the bicycle tracks going all the way back to the jeweller's."

Mrs Harris went to check on the starchy old lady, still snoring away on the grass. "She's spark out, bless her." One of the younger children had put a wild-haired doll next to her, for company.

It was 3:45pm. Mrs Harris dragged her chair out of the shade and sat in the sun for a while, letting the heat of the afternoon soak into her. Rosy, heavily laden sunlight gave everything a soft outline of earthy colours, and she was reminded of a dozen happy summers, long ago.

She watched her teenage sons, one of them spread across the grass quietly driving toy cars with the toddlers, the other on all fours being a valiant steed for the Pimlott girls. She watched them play, and it was as if they were little boys again. She was so proud of them, and loved them so much, that her heart filled with a glow bright enough to hurt.

She lulled into a nap, and although she was only asleep for ten minutes she dreamed a lifetime of memories. In a house she didn't recognise, she met all sorts of people she hadn't seen for decades, all of them pleased to see her but too busy with important clerical work to stop just now. When she woke, she felt a momentary sense of urgency, as if she'd forgotten something vital or left an important job undone, but the sensation quickly passed. Here was the village green, and her sons and her neighbours, and contentment.

Soon it was 4:30pm. Almost as one, the residents of Hillside Drive began to stand up, stretch, collapse their fold-up chairs, with the children moodily awww-ing and do-we-have-to-ing. Most of them dithered slightly, checking the time and exchanging friendly words, delaying the move inside with hugs and handshakes. Mr Jenkins settled into his armchair.

"Would you like Jake to take it back indoors?" said Mrs Harris, leaning down to him.

"No, thank you. I'd like to stay here, actually. Just sit here, if that's OK."

"Yes," smiled Mrs Harris, "of course."

She placed her hand on his for a moment, then joined the general drift back home. She embraced Mrs Pimlott, each of them feeling the tight press of the other's hands on her back. They separated slowly.

"We've had a lovely day, haven't we?" said Mrs Harris softly.

"We have," said Mrs Pimlott the pirate, nodding. "It's been lovely." Arm in arm with Mr Pimlott, she herded her girls into No.77.

Mrs Harris, her boys walking ahead of her, savoured the sensation of her bare feet on the grass, then on the paving slabs that led up to her house, then on the laminate flooring in the hallway by the stairs. Front doors gradually closed, and families gathered on sofas. Out on the grass, the starchy old woman from the end house slept on, her snores like the revs of an outboard motor.

The Harrises sat with Mum's arms around her sons, talking about last year's rainy holiday in Devon and joking about school. Next door, the Pimlotts enjoyed some dreadfully off-key singing from their youngest two daughters. The Greenes were very quiet, hand in hand, the Burtons put on some music and danced in the living room, the Abbots each listened to old favourites on headphones, the Hamiltons told groansome jokes, and the Willises took a selection of strong sleeping pills before settling down.

Comfortable in his armchair, in the sunshine, Mr Jenkins flipped through the old album on his lap, and slid out a faded photo of his Angela. There she was, so young, on the pier at Weston. He smiled at her, the edges of his lips shimmering, and held her to his heart. Behind him, the old woman snored.

Everyone who lived on Hillside Drive was grateful that their street was located less than a hundred miles from the Impact Point. Detonation would occur at 5:01pm, local time, preceded by 57 seconds of extreme winds and gravitational chaos, a period kept short due to the extreme velocity of the incoming mass. An estimated 90 billion tonnes of pulverised rock would be forced into the Earth's atmosphere. All but 0.2% of life on the planet would end within 7 to 8 months.

Above the village green, the amorphous shape in the sky was now larger than the Moon. Soon it was the size of a fist raised against the heavens.

The little princes huddled at the queen's feet, unusually still, their twitchy energy apparently spent for the evening. As Boneweed probed compartments on his cart, a long cascade of thunder rumbled through the ballroom. Rain lashed the tall windows like tendrils of blackclimber.

The king rubbed at his neck and elbows. He managed to relieve the pressure in his gut with a sideways shift and a long, hissing fart. Nevertheless... "Croaknot," he whispered.

His faithful retainer leaned closer, as far as his dodgy hip would bend. "Your Omnipotence?"

"Put tomorrow morning's hunt off until Minnsday. I'm sure the town's jailpit scum won't mind."

"They will rejoice at their temporary reprieve, Your Supremacy. I believe the storyteller is ready to continue."

The king waved a languid gesture of continuance. The queen turned to him with a doubtful look on her face. "Aren't you finding the lack of approved characters confusing, Harlèd?" she said.

"A modern enlightened monarchy like ours must move with the times," he said, voice soured with regret. "Remember what happened to the Lords Of Sandmire. And the Empress-Trinity of the Fire Valleys."

The queen raised her eyebrows thoughtfully.

Different But The Same

I typed the words THE END and sat back. And at that moment, I knew bliss once more. Oh, the precious relief. Oh, the bountiful joy that two little words could bring! The calm, the serenity, the sense of triumph. I sipped my coffee and simply breathed, slow and steady.

Done.

There's a quotation attributed to Dorothy Parker, "I hate writing, I love having written," which she may not actually have said, but sounds like the sort of thing she would say. Anyway, whoever said it, I know exactly what they meant. There's a freedom in *finishing* a long piece of work that's like no other. A sense of having *made* something, of having *created* something through sustained thought and the peculiar alchemy of language.

George Orwell said something equally relevant in the circumstances, he said that writing a book is like enduring a long bout of illness. He was right. Once the thing is finished, and you can finally let go of all the plot threads, characters, themes, phrases, chapters, allusions, metaphors, dialogue, everything that's been buzzing in your head for the last god-know-how-many months, then there's a *physical* reaction. A draining, bodily ache as if every muscle has been held taught for years and then released. For days on end you can't do anything except loll around the house being no use to anyone and feeling half way between flu and clinical depression. Even after – how long would it be, now? – over twenty years as a novelist, this weariness always hits me the same way, a bookend to the unpleasant brain-freeze of staring at an empty page headed 'Chapter One.'

However, end-of-book fatigue is nothing beside the intense anxiety of knowing that people are now going to read the bloody thing. Poke at it, criticise it, assess it. It's like having some anus-mouthed harpy from Social Services sneer at your beloved child. Of course, the last thing I'd ever want to be is one of those prissy, pretentious writers who moan when an editor moves a comma, but even the most pragmatic and market-conscious of us feels the pain of judgement and the hard economic slap of having work boiled down into consumer-facing Product or – even worse – Content. In the *New Grub Street* of life, even the most Jasper Milvain of us has an inner Harold Biffen. Anyway…

For your consideration, a novel. *The Capgras Illusion*. A dark and twisty Cold War thriller with a supernatural edge, about a mid-level government official who is told that his wife has been secretly replaced by a Russian spy. "Nail-biting suspense" the cover will shout. "Jeremy Townshed's best yet!"

It was a day or two before I summoned up the courage to email the new manuscript to my agent, Nigel Flinch at Gull & Pinkloe. Nice bloke, one of those tie-and-plimsoll types with tortoise-shell glasses and a partner who sensibly steers him clear of man buns and sandals. Then, the waiting.

The waiting.

The waiting.

The violent terror between Submission and Verdict.

Yes, yes, yes, very busy, yes, now answer me, answer me.

My phone rang at 10am a few days later. The moment I saw it was Nigel my stomach retreated into my slippers. An agent phones their reaction to a manuscript, rather than emails, for only two reasons. Either 1) your book is a work of outstanding genius, needs revising by no more than a single semi-colon, and will bring you fame and riches forever – this occurs only in the world of dreams. Or 2) your book is shit and this call is a gentle warning full of "I *do* need to re-read it properly"s and "Emily in Publicity is really enjoying it"s to prepare you for a forthcoming editorial attachment slightly longer than *War And Peace*.

I tapped the phone with a shaky finger. "Hi Nigel!" I chirped.

"Jez, how are you?"

"Fine. On the road to recovery, and all that."

He laughed a single 'ha.' "Look, I just wanted to have a quick chat about the new book, have you got a minute?"

Oh shit. Oh fuck. A tone of voice jam-packed with Reason 2. "Yeah, sure." My heart was a runaway steam engine.

"It's, um, err, you've sent me *The Capgras Illusion.*"

"Yes."

"This is a submission, from you to me?"

"Yes."

"As a practical joke?"

"What? Of course not!"

"Because it's not at all funny. Thank goodness Polly in Admin spotted it on my desk before I started sending it out! I'd have looked a complete idiot!"

"It's awful?" I croaked.

"No, it's excellent. Very good indeed, wonderfully real 1950s atmosphere and I love the main character. And the reviews are saying much the same, it had a great write-up in *The Guardian* yesterday."

I paused for a moment. "Nigel, what the bloody hell are you on about? How can it have reviews out? What's wrong with it?"

"What's wrong?" he said. I could hear him leaning forward over his workstation. "You've sent me *The Capgras Illusion* by Marlon Wingley."

"Eh? I'm not using a pseudonym."

"You didn't even put a different title on it!"

"What's wrong with the title?"

"Nothing whatsoever, for Marlon Wingley. You didn't even change the names of half the characters!"

"Nigel, who the fuck is Marlon Wingley?"

"He's the author of *The Capgras Illusion*. Published three weeks ago in paperback by Roman House. Currently number four on the Waterstones fiction bestsellers."

"He picked the same title? Well, I'm not married to it, it's easily changed."

"No, Jez, you're not listening. Bar a few phrases here and there, this is *the same book*. You've sent me Marlon Wingley's book *The Capgras Illusion*, with your name on the front. You've plagiarised it almost word for word, as far as I can see! Why, for heaven's sake? Are you trying to prove a point or something? Like one of those literary terrorists who tweak *Pride And Prejudice* every few years to embarrass all the publishers who turn it down?"

"No!" I protested, barely able to comprehend what I was hearing. "I have never heard of Marlon Wingley—"

"It's his debut novel."

"—and that manuscript, I will have you know, is the result of *nine bloody months' work*! How can it *possibly* be the same as this other book? When did you say it was published?"

"Three weeks ago, the fifteenth."

"Right! I started writing *The Capgras Illusion* in January! *He's* copied *me!*"

"You know perfectly well it doesn't work like that," he sighed wearily. "Roman House's lead times are twelve months minimum, they'll have Wingley's original draft on file dated some time last year. Look, Jez, I know you get a bit of a bee in your bonnet when it comes to anticipating publishers' wish lists, and I know the fads and vagaries of the industry drive you up the wall, but I wish you'd have more faith in your own ability. What you've done here is pointless."

"You're making out it's deliberate!" I cried. "I—I—I can't take this in! It's impossible! I mean, I know they say there's only seven plots, but this is ridiculous. The chances of duplicating eighty-eight thousand, six hundred and twenty words are billions to one! Trillions! It's bloody absurd!"

"Quite," said Nigel. "Now, Jez, have you got anything new for me or not?"

"*That* is new! For fuck's sake! That's nine months of my bloody life sitting there!"

"So that's a 'no' is it? Look, I've got to go into an acquisitions meeting, let's meet up for a drink and a chin-wag next week, yes? And, as and when you've got something original, you know I'll always be keen to see it. Take care, yes?"

I stood motionless at the window of my cupboard-like office, phone in hand, staring out at next door's bins, for about a week and a half.

There is a well-known aphorism in the world of book publishing: *different, but the same*. It describes what mainstream publishers want to see in their inboxes, what they're most willing to buy, namely something which is *both* entirely fresh and original *and* almost exactly the same as many previous successes. The new blockbuster for all readers of bestseller X; book A meets smash hit B for a new generation; the brilliant new novel for fans of celebrity author C. That sort of thing. Nigel and I have never exactly been eye to eye on this subject. He thinks it's solidly commercial common sense. I think it's stifling, defeatist shite which does nothing but encourage the dumbing down of society.

Yes, OK, sure, of course, almost everything new is inspired by *something* else, and of course, inevitably, unavoidably, huge overlaps are commonplace in all art (that's what creates genre, right?) but inspiration is not duplication. Actual duplication. Roland Barthes said the author is dead, not the author is a photocopier. What Nigel was telling me was impossible.

Naturally, in my shocked state, I thought maybe he was just winding me up, so I hurried to the nearest bookshop with lead weights in my gut. There it was, on the table beside the window display, sandwiched between a thriller about a kidnapped wife and a thriller about a wife who plans a bank heist with her kidnapped husband – *The Capgras Illusion* by Marlon Wingley.

I picked it up, turned it over, flicked through the pages. "The best debut I've read in years" – *London Tonite*. "Absolutely nerve-tingling" – *The Bookgobbler* review blog. Chapter 1 – "Gerald Masters smiled up at Brenda as she placed the coffee cup in front of him, but her usual reply, that soft look of indulgence he knew so well and loved so much, was missing this morning…"

My words. Mine. Chapter 2, Chapter 3, Chapter 27. Those metaphorical lead weights plopped out of my arse and onto the floor. I felt hollow. Empty. I turned to the author photo on the inside back cover. Younger than me. Trendier than me. Better looking than me. Fucker. Bastard fucker. "MARLON WINGLEY spent ten years troubleshooting on behalf of a major international aid organisation before turning his hand to storytelling. He lives in a riverside cottage in Surrey with his partner, their two young children and an unruly Yorkshire terrier. *The Capgras Illusion* is his first novel."

A drip of my anguish splashed the cover. I hastily pulled myself together, put the book down and went to catch the bus home. As streets slid by, I couldn't help but think this duplication had to be deliberate. Didn't it? Somehow? There had to be some sort of trick. Some sort of scam. It just didn't make sense!

I did some digging on Mr Wingley. His online presence was minimal, his website bland, his PR uneventful.

Had he hacked my laptop and nicked the manuscript? Impossible, timing-wise, as Nigel had pointed out. Had he hacked my laptop, nicked the manuscript and travelled back in time to submit it to Roman House? Oooh, what a good idea for a story!

I felt numb. And very, very, very angry. And extremely bewildered.

Get a grip, I told myself eventually. Get a grip or you'll go mad.

There's two ways this can go. You can either pursue this bastard fucker like all the furies of Hell, track him down, demand an explanation, smack him with a shovel and bury him under his bloody riverside cottage…

The sheer workload involved in vengeance was enough to rule *that* out. I could go to see him. Talk to him. And say what, exactly? Even the best case scenario meant an authorship battle spiralling into litigation for which I had no resources whatsoever...

Or... you can accept the situation and move on...

Move on. Because I didn't have time for this. For fuck's sake, I'd just had nine bloody months' work flushed down the pan and I needed to earn some money! I had no choice but to move on. Come to terms with it. Just a difficulty, just a setback, a boulder dropped into my path on life's potholed, piss-drenched alleyway. I'd had plenty of setbacks in my time, hadn't I? Plenty of heart-crushing disappointments? U'd survived the, right? I could survive this one too. A bloody weird one, granted, but This Too Shall Pass, right? It was one of those mind-boggling coincidences you hear about, an Aristotelian infinite monkeys moment, producing not *Hamlet* but *The Capgras Illusion*!

OK.

So...

I had some undeveloped ideas tucked away in my notebooks. I was confident I could produce a new manuscript in, say, three months, if I knuckled down and ignored all thoughts of literary quality. Sort out all the rough edges later, once a publisher was onboard. Forget artistry, just thump out the words. Two thousand a day, every weekday, allowing a week at the start for plotting, a week at the end for reading through and correcting the worst bits. Doable. A nightmare, but doable. It's what Ian Fleming did, voluntarily.

Cut to: eleven weeks, three days later – "THE END."

I almost wept with happiness. Another thriller, this time a little more psychological, with an is-it-real-or-is-it-in-his-head? angle. *I'm Looking At You Now*. A man who enjoys playing practical jokes, and travels a lot for his job, leaves a little calling card at every hotel in which he stays. On the bathroom mirror he writes "I am watching you" such that the letters only appear when a new guest uses the shower and gets the place all steamy. He has a good laugh thinking of the frights he must give people – until a whole series of similar messages start appearing in his home, in his car and at his workplace…

I was pleased with it, all things considered. It read OK, once I'd ironed out some of the haste-induced shittiness. Good strong hook, lots of unexpected consequences, a brutal climactic chase across a huge building site. Not bad.

I emailed it to Nigel with my heart fluttering like a butterfly in a wind tunnel. I turned my phone off for a couple of days while I slept, watched some favourite films, and slept some more. With rain battering the world outside, I switched on again – two missed calls, no messages. I decided to wait until he called back. When he did, I almost jumped out of my skin.

"Have you been away?" said Nigel.

"Yes," I said cheerily, "a long weekend in the country with some friends."

"Nice. Feeling refreshed?"

"Absolutely."

"Good, then perhaps you'd like to stop sending me other people's books?"

Ice replaced my blood. "What?"

"*Here's Looking At You*, whatever you've called it, I got two chapters in and was really enjoying it, very quick-paced and readable, and then I twigged why the chap's antics seemed familiar. I'd read them before. Fifteen, twenty years ago, was it? *Messages In The Mirror* by Walter Evan Prentis. Quite a hit in its day."

Seconds became months. "What?"

"It's been out of print for years, is that why you thought I wouldn't know it?"

Months became decades. "Is this a joke? Are you taking the piss?"

"I could ask you the same thing."

"You're telling me *this* manuscript is *also* identical to someone else's?"

"Yes, that is indeed what I'm telling you. Bar the title. Your title is better, I'll give you that. Oh, and some of the character names, and the first chapter ends at a slightly different point. Did you change it to put me off the scent? Look, Jez… are you OK? Have you got money troubles again? Are you… under stress over something?"

"Yes," I said, my voice tiny, "I am feeling stressed, all of a sudden, yes, I am, yes. You don't want my book, then? You don't want it? You can't sell it? It's no good?"

"Is *is* good. But it isn't yours."

Shrinking, feeble. "You don't want it? You can't sell it?"

There was a long pause. I could hear someone battering a computer keyboard in the background. "You know the answer to that, Jez. Look, we really must have that drink some time, soon, thrash things out, yes? In the meantime… don't do this again, OK?… That's enough now."

A microscopic dot upon a microscopic dot. "I'm sorry."

It took a few days to locate a second hand copy of *Messages In The Mirror* by Walter Evan Prentis, but I found one listed by a bookseller in Bath. Rather than wait for the post, I reserved it and got there just before the shop closed for the day.

I love old paperbacks. Their slightly dusty smell, their browned and freckled pages, their bleached spines and colour-muted covers. Unlike their sibling hardbacks – tough, rigid, built to last – they're vulnerable, their chances of survival limited without an owner's care. Yet here they are, delicate but unbowed, hanging on, their inner worlds still a-flicker. Old paperbacks are normally such evocative, comforting things.

This one wasn't. On the train home I steadily turned the pages. Every paragraph familiar. Almost every sentence. Even the positions of full stops and em dashes, duplicated pronouns, identical adverbial phrases.

It was impossible.

It was impossible.

Had I read it in the past, and forgotten? Had I somehow dragged it from the depths of my memory? In precise and unerring detail?

No, I fucking well hadn't! My book, my work, had been stolen from me! Fuck knows how, but someone, somewhere, somehow, was sticking two fingers up at me. Up yours, you talentless hack! It was like marrying the most beautiful girl in the world and then watching her tear off a rubber mask, ha ha sucker I'm really the corpse of a Nazi child murderer!

Who was doing this? Was someone doing this? How could someone do this? It was a long time before the boiling stew of anger, disbelief and paranoia in my head settled down enough for me to think clearly. For days I tried to convince myself that the last few months were nothing but a fever dream.

I slapped myself to wake up. No, already wide awake.

For a while, my delirious brain said I must be a fictional character in a comic book or a novel or a TV episode, the puppet of some cruel literary-themed villain. Either that, or I was dead and being tortured by the ancient Cthulhu gods of bookselling.

When more rational thoughts prevailed at last, I tried working out, mathematically, the actual real-life chances of two entire book manuscripts being almost exactly duplicated. The odds, wow, gosh, this is interesting, were in the tera-giga-trillions, a mere few hundred million tera-giga-trillions, in fact.

If only to preserve my teetering sanity, I reasoned thus: if we live in a multiverse and/ or we live in an infinite space of infinite possibilities, then presumably I simply happened to be living in the tiny, quantum, ato-reality in which something *staggeringly* unlikely has happened to me. Twice.

It was an almost laughable thing to accept but... again, what else could I do? Seriously, what else could I do? Logic-defying things *do* happen in the world, things that make absolutely no sense at all – bumblebees fly, ice baths are good for you, people vote for the Conservative Party.

With an aching heart, and with the bitterest grief eating at my soul, I took a deep breath and started again. I started again.

I did the due diligence. I settled on a terrific idea, plotted it out carefully, and then – with infinite care and leaving no figurative stone unturned – I scoured every source of information I could get my hands on: databases, library catalogues, websites, reference books, everything, until I was *absolutely certain*, beyond all possible doubt, that my idea had never seen paper, celluloid or digital file before. Ever.

Cut to: nineteen weeks, six days later. THE END. I'd grown a beard and my personal hygiene had, on this occasion, regrettably fallen short of the high standards expected.

The premise was a kind of sci-fi allegory, a twist on a prisoner-of-war story: several dozen men, women and children wake up one morning to discover they've been dumped in a series of filthy shelters in the middle of a bleak, muddy expanse surrounded by an unscalable wall. They're naked, freezing cold and have no idea where they are, or why, beyond the obvious fact that they're prisoners.

They're scared witless, not only by their situation but by the fact that all memories of their lives up to this point appear to have been deliberately blurred. One or two of the group gravitate into leadership positions and, in an effort to raise morale, set off to find an escape route.

They are interrupted by a couple of huge, monstrous creatures who appear via a sliding opening in the wall. The prisoners plead for an explanation of their plight, and better treatment. The creatures completely ignore them, talking only to each other in a strange, musical language. They leave food for the prisoners and depart. Have aliens invaded? Is there an interstellar war going on? Have the prisoners been taken to another planet?

The find-an-escape group manage to get outside the walled compound. They sneak into the creatures' dwelling, an enormous, weirdly shaped structure full of sealed chambers. Then, in one of these chambers – shock horror! – they witness the creatures gleefully butchering and cooking a prisoner! They race back to the compound!

Giant middle-of-the-book twist – we realise that the prisoners aren't human beings, they're pigs. The creatures are human farmers. The story reverses itself – how did the pigs become intelligent? Why? Can they find a way to communicate with the humans? If they do, how will the humans react?

Then, after many failed attempts, the pigs succeed! They manage to talk to the farmers! But! Terrifying reveal at the end

– this is the year 1625, the pigs are deemed possessed by demons and burnt as witches.

A rattling good yarn, full of things to say about the human condition! I emailed it to Nigel, had a bath, went to the pub for the afternoon, came back and perused the latest publishing industry headlines. Petrel Press Title On Hold After Plagiarism Claim. Somebody called Veronica Kettlewen was causing a row because her novel *We Regard The Stars*, about... a group of pigs... who become intelligent... on a farm... in 1625... published Monday... immediately challenged... by publishers of *El destino de las cabras* by Enzo A Gonzales, published a fortnight ago... which is exactly the same... except goats...

One week later, an email from Nigel. Not a call this time, an email. An email effusive in its praise for my considerable gifts as a writer, declaring with heart-rending reluctance that an agent's professional influence in the market is finite, expressing the certainty that my career would flourish thanks to a fresh perspective, and jauntily wishing me the very best of luck in all my endeavours. Fifteen years. Dumped in three, four... five sentences.

I didn't respond. What would have been the point?

This Too Shall Pass. Except, it didn't.

Some years ago, I was on a three-writer panel at a mystery/ crime/ horror fiction convention. One of the questions the audience asked was 'what scares *you*?' Panelist 1 got in quick with 'reviewers!' and got a big laugh. Panelist 2 lost their attention with some crap about losing the art of storytelling. I honestly can't remember what I said, but I know what I wanted to say: screaming into the wind, that's what scares me. Being unheard. Being invisible. A speck of dust lost in infinity. Irrelevant. Forgotten.

I couldn't face searching for a new agent. The thought of being at the bottom of the ladder again, sweating my way through vicious knife fights in the Pit Of Unsolicited Submission made me feel physically sick. So did the thought of waiting months for politely terse replies in which assorted Tims and Jennifers thanked me so much but didn't *quite* love the work enough to make an offer or didn't *quite* have a clear enough vision of its core metrics going forward. As if it was the sole purpose of my life to precision-please them. Me, in print before half of them were fucking born and every bit their equal in literary judgement, thank you very much!

No, for the time being I'd go back to basics. Refresh the palate, as it were, with some short stories. It crossed my mind to self-publish a volume of them, although the relentless promotional effort required was extremely disheartening. I doubted I had the skill to start battling algorithms and micro-attention spans. Or the energy. Or the guts, quite frankly. Think about it later.

No, I decided, I'll just shut myself away from the world for a little while, shut out the madness and come up with some solid ideas, something as yet unimaginable. See what happens. Let the proverbial chips fall where they may. Something would turn up. It always had, in the past, when times were hard. I'd make Mr Micawber look like a pessimistic old git.

I flicked through some old notebooks, went for a few walks, lay on the floor for a few hours. A month later, I had a decent collection of strong opening lines...

As soon as I opened the living room curtains that Tuesday morning and saw a unicorn standing on the front lawn, I knew reality was fucked... An exercise in magic realism. It is discovered that human eco-negligence has not only choked the biosphere and wrecked the climate, but has also torn the fabric of space-time itself. Our hero, an ordinary guy living on an ordinary street in – let's say, maybe Manchester or Bournemouth – witnesses the slow 'surrealisation' of the planet, with life becoming gradually more bizarre over the course of several years, until he himself turns into something very odd I haven't quite decided on yet.

I made nine kills today... A zombie apocalypse tale in which the dead don't become ravening, inarticulate monsters but ultra-nice, ultra-neat-and-tidy sticklers for the rules. They kill anything living because living beings are too unpredictable and disobedient. A nightmare dystopia of rigid conformity and blandness! Our hero is a lone survivor, picking off zombies with home-made weapons wherever she can. Plot twist – there are other survivors after all, who blend in with the zombies by acting like them, and she's been inadvertently killing them too!

Why had it never occurred to anyone that our global civilisation would be ended so quickly and so completely, not by disaster, disease, or war, but by a blank piece of paper?... Another end-of-the-world tale. (I seemed to be developing a theme here, probably a psychological reflection of my current state of mind.) The world wakes up one day to find that every piece of paper, old or new, has become blank. So have all computer records, and anything storing information using letters and numbers. New records can be created, but all the old ones are gone forever. Without documentation economies collapse, laws don't exist any more, concepts like ownership and authority are kaput. Actually, thinking about it, this is a story about optimism, in which the characters quickly learn the benefits of co-operation and mutual protection, creating a new society from the ground up.

Mr Thompson kept a clone of himself in the attic, and violently mistreated it… A horror story with a surprise ending – you think this is a lone nutter with serious issues and access to high technology, but it turns out that almost everyone is doing exactly the same thing.

The crumbling manuscript we found in the wall correctly predicted what happened today… Spooky Kneale-ish shenanigans when a young couple, renovating an old house, find a document dated 1908 which correctly predicts many world events. And their own unexpected deaths!

I had plenty of others too: one about a time travelling archaeologist who discovers he's digging up his own bones; one about a woman who replaces her children with androids and soon prefers them to the real thing; one about a smartphone app which lets you choose real-life fates for the real-life arseholes of your choice. A mixed bag of ideas, but some quite good ones here and there, I thought.

Before I set about tap-tap-tapping into the early hours, turning them into finished work, I combed through every piece of short fiction on my shelves, hundreds of them, just to reassure myself that none of these ideas were the Ghosts Of Reading Past. No, nothing in this collection which even comes close to one of my new plots, and nothing in this one, or this one, or this one, from one end of the shelf to the other. No, I had not dredged any narratives from the deep recesses of my memory.

Good. Right.

Then, obviously, a thorough double-check online. I felt perfectly calm. I had well over two dozen different outlines here. If one or two of them turned out to be pre-owned? Not a problem. Or even the majority? Perfectly liveable-with. All of them? Every last one? Yeah, right, if that happens the cosmos really *has* picked me, personally, to crap on from a great height.

Strange Earthrise Over Bournemouth by Julius Phipps, 1977. *Plague Of The Agreeables* by Annabel Strim, "author of the award-winning *Digging My Own Bones*," 2018. "Top 10 Best Stories About Societal Breakdown Caused By The Blanking Of All Paper," buzzload.com, 2021. "I'm working on a novel about parental anxiety," says Booker shortlistee Toby Hulkington, "in which mechanisms replace offspring." *Tales Of The Peculiar* magazine, August 1965, *Automated Revenge Inc.* by Nancy K. Zoom.

The Futurist's Owl by Norman Trotter, 2022.

All Our Trolls Are In Revolt by Edward Plennary, 1927.

How Stare The Sheep by Belinda Otomo, 2008.

My Razor Cutteth by Bill Volta, 1990.

Six And Nine Make Five by Cassie Clerkly, 1953.

Dead Men Shoot Back by Patrick Markham Harries, 1959.

Tumble Down The Hillock by F. D. Whick

The classic *Go Forth To Jingtin*; the acclaimed locked room mysteries of Ivan Westinghouse; James W. McGuinnock; Felix Pert; Ellis Oiling; *The Seventh Wife Of Alison Storm*; *Ghosts Over Derby*; Annie Dawn Tregowan; the *Ring Pods Of Karbo* sequence; *Brides Of The Lost Schooner*; Trevor Hug's award-winning *Moonings*; *My Son The Minotaur*; the *All Buses Blue* series; *The Teatime Poems Of Ezra Sands volume 4*; *Singing The Toads Back Home*; *My Life As A Puddle*; *Practical Wasp-keeping*; *Ding Dong Said The Pope*; *The Falling*; *The Squirming*; *The Girl In The Orchard*; *The Rise-upping*; *Functional Use Of The Mixed Metaphor In Jacobean Verse*. And on, and on.

Done! Done! Done! All of it, ALL OF IT, a hundred times over! Done!

What in God's name is happening?

What the fuck is happening to me?

I cheated. I went to an AI bot, thing, whateveryoucallit. Write me a 5000 word story, on any subject, which expresses a completely original idea, or plot device, or fictional situation, which has never, in any way whatsoever, appeared in any written or transmitted form before.

Now it happens one evening I am on the corner of Forty-second Street and Broadway, and who do I see but August Wilson, who is known as Lucky Wilson to one and all as he is, more than somewhat, a gambler of very little success. Lucky Wilson is a fat guy, and gabby, and mostly he is wearing raggedy clothes and busted shoes. He speaks as follows:

"Well," says Lucky Wilson, "I am in possession of a system for the numbers that cannot possibly miss." He is also one hundred per cent sucker and announces possession of a sure-fire system on a weekly basis… and so on and so on—

No! For fuck's sake! That's just copying Damon Runyon! Try again!

and so on and so on—

What? That's faux-Jane Austen, that's worse! Again!

and so on and so on—

Bloody Dickens!

and so on and so on—

Conan Doyle! Angela Carter! Melville! Amis! William sodding Burroughs!

and so on and so on—

Iambic fucking pentameter? Are you fucking JOKING?

It was dark outside. The only light in the room was the cold glare of the laptop screen. A strange sensation crept through me like a hundred tiny knives, as my hands trembled over the keys.

Go on, then. Say something. Type something. Tell us something new. Start with a capital letter. An 'E' maybe…? Or a 'P'…? What words? From the millions that exist… what words?

Is there nothing left? Has every possible combination of words already been formed, over and over again?

Is there nothing left to DO or SAY or BE that millions, millions, millions of people haven't *done* or *said* or *been* a million times before? Is there nothing conceivable left unexpressed? No fresh thought not burnt out years ago? No clever enterprise not already beaten to an over-saturated market? Has *everything,* has every *variation* of everything passed into yesterday, discarded by bored and jaded minds?

Is there nothing left to create at all? Is it all recycling itself forever in a slow, bilious re-digestion, every grimy lump deconstructed and star rated? Can anything of any meaning be plucked from this endless, infinite info-havoc?

Was I recycled too? Vomiting nonsense until death?

I felt myself fade into oblivion, shrivel into grey, ashen nothingness. I was deafened by the howling roar of a billion voices, all of them shouting, yelling, SCREAMING! None of them making a sound. Everyone just PISSING INTO THE OCEAN!

Wait.

No, WAIT!

What about everything I'd done before this whole nightmare began? Years of work! There, on my bookshelves, copies of all twenty-three titles, published over a period of twenty-five years. Some of them had done moderately well, some had sunk without trace, but *there they were*. Undeniable.

My contribution to the world. A modest one… but *my* contribution. My babies. My legacy. My existence.

Except that—

They weren't. One by one, checking, checking. Why hadn't I checked before? Why hadn't anyone told me before?

This book of mine: also written and published in 1899 as *The Far Mountains* by Tito Knowles, and in 1922 as *To The Summit* by Gregory Juques, and in 1941 as *The Mountaineers* by Peter McDingle.

And this book of mine: issued before as *Diamond Heist* (1990), *The Getaway* (2002), *Escape The Law* (2012).

And this book of mine: repeating every detail of paperbacks from 1938, 1955, 1957, 1972, 2000, 2020.

No, no, no, no, no. Now it was happening fucking backwards! Had I just missed it? All this time? Why hadn't I…? Why hadn't someone…? What the actual FUCK?

There was nothing left. I had done nothing, said nothing. Was nothing. I had wasted my life! My whole life!

Wait.

No, WAIT!

There were still words. Yes. Single, individual words. I could invent one!

Yes, yes, one last chance. OK, OK, it can be anything. Any splatter of letters I like, just so long as I give it a meaning. Yes. Any old shit. I'll just paddle my hands on the keyboard and spew the word onto the page.

rupdgwiaowmbtqldertsstom

There. That's my word. My totally new, made-up word. Right, good, now let's prove it, let's do an online search. Give me a minute.

YOU ARE FUCKING KIDDING ME!

There it is – "rupdgwiaowmbtqldertsstom." It's there in a fucking short horror story by some pond scum called Gadz. Who the FUCK is he? How the FUCK did he write MY word?

And look at it, this short story! Look! It's about a writer who goes out of his mind because everything he writes has already been written. It's insane! You couldn't make it up! Although, apparently, Jesus H Fucking Christ, this bastard DID make it up! Apparently! This fucking PARASITE has ruined my last chance!

What can I do? What the hell can I do? What the bloody fucking damnation in hell am I supposed to do now? Eh?

I know, I'll just stop. I'll just fucking STOP! Nobody can beat me to THAT! They've all PRODUCED stuff, they've all CREATED stuff, well, I'm going to do the opposite. I'm going to stop, now, I'm going to pick up this bloody laptop and I am going to hurl it out of the fucking window and watch it smash to pieces in the street! Then NOBODY can beat me! NOBODY! Because I'M the one who's stopping, ME, ME, I'm the one who'll ge

Lightning flashed garish, angular shapes across the castle ballroom. The tall windows streamed, turning every momentary glimpse of the mountains into a shimmering cascade.

The servant Croaknot stood beside the thrones as straight as his weak spine could bear, gazing out into the darkness. His wizened hand touched at his papery cheeks and the three vertical scars which were the sigil of his rank. His spoke wistfully, as if breathing an antique prophecy. "The skywater falls so plumply tonight, Your Mightiness."

The king wasn't listening. He, and the queen, and the little princes, and all the courtiers seated behind them, were focussed only on Boneweed and the dreamy haze into which he was gradually leading them. Their eyes were puddles of ink on clean white paper.

Boneweed opened another book, this one even older and dustier. The creamy-yellow pages crackled as they turned. "Come," he said through his unsettling smile, two spidery fingers gently beckoning. "Slip into the spell of words. They alone are our concern tonight, for enchantment lurks in their arrangements. Come."

The king sat forward. Now his back was hurting. Must be this hard throne. "Continue, Citizen…"

You'll Always Walk Alone

Every night, at bedtime, after he'd finished reading a chapter of his current book, Mum would come to turn his light off and snuggle him up tight. Then he would close his eyes and wish, wish, wish that tonight would be the night he'd sleep forever. With all his heart, with fingers entwined, he wished for eternal rest, never to wake again.

It's not that he wanted to die. Not die, exactly. Wouldn't death be painful? It looked painful on telly, full of screams and groaning. He didn't want that. He just wanted to sleep and to exist only in sleep. If he could just stay here, under the covers, warm and alone, in a personal, perpetual limbo, that would be enough.

He wanted time itself to stop, so that tomorrow could never arrive.

But every morning, without fail, consciousness would come to re-chill his mind. For a moment, he'd be suspended in the shallow grave of oblivion, a ghostly bliss before memory's sharp bite. Sometimes, as he woke up, it felt to him as if sleep had slipped carelessly through his grasp like water, as if he'd fumbled its delicate web and let it dissolve into the past through some terrible mistake.

And then, his first emotion of each day, a hollow burst of dread, gutting him like a blade. His nightly wish ignored again. Or maybe, he'd think, in last minute desperation, perhaps, time *could* stop right now *instead*? Right *now*. That would be OK too. Stop before the day began, before the clock struck, the bell tolled, the hourglass turned.

"Paul and William! Getting up time!" Mum called from the bottom of the stairs. She always called from the bottom of the stairs, exactly five minutes after his older brother Paul was already up and in the bathroom, exactly ten minutes before the sound of Paul unhooking the bathroom latch forced William out of bed and into the empty bathroom's lingering fart-soap-brother-mist.

He kept a stubby, bitten pencil on a shelf, for crossing off each yesterday on his Green Shield Stamps calendar, sellotaped under the light switch by his door. Yesterday, Sunday, October 8th, 1972. Black line through it, gone. Today, Monday 9th. Clean clothes day, luncheon meat school dinner day.

He squinted in the harsh light from the bathroom's dangling bulb, and his feet felt cold on the scuffed lino (step white square, black, white, black, tap soap one, two, three). A popping, metallic warmth came from the immersion tank in the airing cupboard.

The plumbing gurgled. William listened, as still as a statue. The goblin was stirring, fitfully, quietly.

The goblin was invisible, a haunting in the walls. Invisible, intangible, inaudible. Yet, he could feel it in the sudden coldness on the landing and in the glancing touch of scratchy fingers under the table. He could see it in the suddenly-creasing wallpaper and in the corners where shadows shouldn't be. He could hear it in the ache of floorboards and the sobbing of dark tears in the night.

It lived in the fabric of the house, in its bricks, its wood, its plastic. Gurgling, creaking, always vigilant, making its funny toys for funtime. The rhythm of the day was the jittering pulse of the goblin's brain a-thinking.

They could all feel the goblin's presence – William, his brother Paul, his mum and his dad – but nobody had ever seen it, and nobody ever spoke of it. To talk about it (bad) was to speed up the music of its dance. To plot against it (worse) was to invite all its most hilarious toys to the dinner table, to summon them out of the plaster and the concrete, and nobody wanted that, not again. Rebellious behaviour (worstest of all) might cause the goblin to animate a little stick-dwarf with piercing yellow eyes, send it running through a doorway, cackling.

The goblin lived here to play with its pet family. It watched them through every raw vibration of the house, it weaved a regular funtime for each member of the family, each person in its collection.

They sat at the kitchen table, William and his brother, eating cornflakes. The room still held an echo of yesterday's laundry, the weekly humid fug of washing powder. William wasn't keen on cornflakes but Mum wouldn't buy Ricicles or Coco Pops. Too expensive. His school friend Trev got Puffa Puffa Rice for breakfast. William sprinkled on more sugar.

Coats on, dinner money, oh look at the state of your shoes. Dad was busy in the front room, with the curtains closed, trying not to yell at the slithering patterns of the carpet, the furniture jabbing all around him. Mum stood at the open front door, her face fixed, letting out the heat and fumbling to light a cigarette, until the boys were at the end of the road.

William walked with his brother as far as West Street. They played musical burps when nobody was in earshot, breath-clouds trailing in the stark air. When his brother turned right for the Secondary Modern, William turned left towards the Primary.

Assembly, Maths, English, break, double Science, dinner, Geography, Football on the sports field. Football was his least favourite thing at school, nothing but mud and freezing cold (last term's report: "…William is very good at being where the ball isn't.") His favourites were English and Art ("…despite his rather morbid imagination.")

All the time, all day, fearful of going home, not wanting to go home. Watching the hours tick past on the classroom clock (big hand on three so third finger, tap one, two, three). Watching the wintery sky, grey to white to grey to charcoal and darkness. The smell of shoes and PE kit, tick tock. The insincere warmth of lights switched on mid-afternoon, tick tock. A couple of times, he rubbed away a tickle on his skin, a slight irritation like the walking of a tiny spider. Messages from home, from the goblin, to let him know it was watching.

He had an inkling that others' lives were different, somehow, but he couldn't really grasp the idea. Couldn't ask. Rebellious behaviour (worstest).

Home time, the screech of chairs, the boom of teachers. He left alongside his friend Trev, and Trev's mum picked them up in her Cortina. She drove an MG-B in the summer, her feet bare on the pedals. He knew, from things Trev had said, that she thought he was a strange lad. Bit odd. He liked the way her hair fluffed blonde and floaty over the top of the driver's seat.

His house was on the way to Trev's, so it was no bother to drop him off right by his gate. He waved the car into the distance. Home, normality.

His house looked the same as all the others in the street, four windows at the front. Houses closer to school had three, and houses up by Trev's had six. They'd moved in when he was five years old, so he'd lived half his life in it and couldn't remember living anywhere else. Nice family, very quiet, keep themselves to themselves, said the neighbours.

Mum was in the kitchen. As William came in, his battered shoes clomping on the hard floor, she looked away from the window and its view of the tiny garden outside. The plastic washing line flapped in the cold breeze. The grass wanted cutting. She smiled at him but her lips didn't move. They stood together, in silence, feeling the room draw breath, then hearing a new funny toy above them, up in the bathroom, shifting its weight, something bulky and scratching. They felt the walls giggle but they dared not speak.

The slow clunk of the front door said Dad was home from the depot. He trudged up the stairs to wash the smell of diesel and hydraulics off himself. Mum's face tilted upward slightly, her mouth set tight. Warnings were rebellion (worstest). They heard the bulky something thrash and strike, and they heard Dad whimper. Remember, please, don't cry out, daddy, husband, don't cry out, you know some toys play nicer than others.

William watched telly in the living room. *Pardon My Genie* (funny) and *Magpie* (boring). Paul returned from Train Club. For tea, there would be grilled sausies with boiled potatoes and boiled veg (nice).

William went to his room. Some funny toys were parading in a ring above his wardrobe, little hairy ones with wheels. He was painfully worried for a moment, but they merged into the wall and were gone. He dried his eyes, opened his school bag, slung his football kit into a corner and got out his Maths workbook. Homework was five sums, not too hard apart from the fourth one, which had fractions in it. Farts from the Devil's arse, Trev called them. William got what looked like the right answer in the end: seven over twenty-one is three, because three times seven is twenty-one. Three, right.

The Maths workbook went back in the bag and he picked up last week's *Cor!!* but it all washed past his eyes because his thoughts were elsewhere. As the pages turned a nameless state of worry began to gnaw at him, because Mum hadn't said tea was ready.

Routine was the rusty mechanism that balanced the house, keeping the goblin's brain as un-poked as possible, helping calm the bloodlust of funtimes. Dad was home, Paul was home. Mum hadn't said tea was ready (thumb to fingertips, one, two, three, four, three, two, one).

William's feet jittered nervously. He heard himself taking breaths (one, two, three, four, three, two, one, repeat, repeat, repeat). There was an eerie silence everywhere.

"Tea's ready!" Mum's voice jittered nervously too. He could hear reluctance. Have tea anyway. Time for tea. Have tea anyway.

He and Paul thundered downstairs. At the kitchen table, they ate hungrily. Where was Dad? The sausies were a little bit burned but they were still nice. Mum sat and picked at the skin around her finger nails, scratching off tiny strips and flicking them at the floor. Her eyes kept darting to the back door and her lips moved in strange twitches. Eventually, she pointed to her untouched plate. "I'm not hungry, you two have it." William silently took a sausie and some veg. So did Paul, his face grim.

William looked at Dad's tea, getting cold. He looked up at Mum, whose silent face screamed loud enough to shatter glass. Where was Dad? William finished what was on his plate and placed his knife and fork together neatly.

Mum returned to the kitchen window. Her hands gripped the edge of the sink, then dug for a cigarette and a match. William couldn't tell if she was staring at her reflection, thrown into the glass by the florescent strip overhead, or at the pitch dark of the night beyond.

In the living room, he pulled his legs up onto the sofa. He idly plucked at a loose thread on his sock, near the top where the elastic bit had gone slack. His brother put the telly back on and cla-dunked the channel buttons over to *Nationwide* (boring).

There was a peculiar tremble in the ceiling, like a tightening of suppressed anger. Small footsteps hopped around the wall behind them. On the screen, there was a report about fraudulent gas fitters.

William suddenly felt the sofa rise a hand's width off the floor. He wedged himself in a bit. A thunderous banging from upstairs made them jump, doors being slammed. After a few seconds, the noise stopped as violently as it had started.

He watched the telly. "And that's all from us this Monday evening, so it's goodnight." Logo, fanfare-y music.

The smell of Mum's cigarettes diffused through the house. She paced the ground floor, slowly at first, in and out of the hallway, but with increasing speed. Where was Dad?

A wave of ice cold air cascaded through the room. The sofa bumped down against the floorboards and was still once more.

"Programmes tonight on BBC1, in a moment there's another case for…" The contents of all the cupboards in the kitchen began to rattle and skip. Paul got up and pressed the channel buttons. ITV. *Money For Nothing* (silly). "The five pound question, Doreen, is: what is the capital city of Thailand? What is the capital city… of Thailand?" The kitchen cupboard doors began to thud too. William heard the sink taps turn on and off, on and off, on and off. "Your time starts – now."

In his head and stomach, he felt the whole room suddenly flip upside down, but nothing physically changed or moved. He clung to the sofa as if he might drop down onto the ceiling at any moment. He could tell Mum felt it too, because she quietly sat in one of the armchairs, breathing hard and plucking the last cigarette from the packet.

"Peking." Ding! "No, I'm so sorry, m'love, the answer is in fact Bangkok. That reminds me, I've got a hospital appointment." Laughter.

"I saw Dad in the garden," said Mum, her voice low and strained, as if each word was torn from her throat by force. "He's not there now."

William stared at her. There was something in her eyes, the same hard vacancy she wore whenever the toys at her funtime had been really bad to her. He began to feel a surge of morning dread, as if he'd just woken (repeat, repeat, repeat). He tightened his jaw to stop the tremble in his lower lip.

On the TV, Shirley from Swindon was this week's contestant in the Big Money round. Applause.

"Where is he?" said Paul. Don't forget, brother, son, speak with care!

"He…" she breathed. With care, mother! "They played too rough. I think it was an accident." Her whole manner was sharp and clenched, holding back explosions. William got a sick, liquid feeling in his chest, and his eyes started to swim.

Broken! Broken! Toys tipped out of the box. Everything spoiled. If naughty goblins can't take care of pets, then they shan't have any!

Mum dragged terror from her cigarette, her fingers drumming on the armrest. Shirley from Swindon won a brand new family car. Good night everyone.

Paul got up and stalked into the kitchen. Mum followed him, huffing smoke, her words like splintered metal. "He's not there! Paul!" The cooker and the cupboards rattled and gibbered around them.

William couldn't stop his face from scrunching. Remember, show no weakness, brother, youngest, it excites their blood. He pulled a cushion to himself and held it like a shield, half covering his head.

Sudden clatters and whirs announced the arrival of funny toys. Lots of them. He peeked out from behind his shield, his stomach knotting at the thought of funtime, but they merely wandered around the floor and walls and ceiling, ignoring each other, flexing their appendages. Some were new to him, with shiny lenses and unstained teeth. Others made him flinch from memories. They circulated, clacking their sharp edges and making racing car noises.

Mum walked decisively through to the hall, her last cigarette drawn to a tiny stub between her fingers. She recoiled as the front door handle hissed and snapped at her, and the letterbox barked itself hoarse. William felt his heartbeat as a sped-up shoreline in his ears. If they'd had a phone in their house like Trev, he wondered, would he hear Mum tapping at the clicky things and saying 'dead' like detectives did on telly.

Mum returned to the armchair and Paul returned to the other end of the sofa. Both were brittle with the relentless defeat of seconds, minutes, hours, days, weeks, months, years. William didn't know what to do. Learned instinct told him to be still and silent. He found it difficult to think, with all these funny toys in the room.

Suddenly, the toys stopped in their tracks. Those with eyes nervously swivelled them about. The rattling noises in the kitchen ceased and for a half minute or more the only sound came from the TV.

"It's the taste that says tea!"

"Here, put the kettle on, Frank."

"Potley's. Britain's Best Cuppa."

A glass ornament lifted off the sideboard and whipped across the room to smash above the cold gas fire. William ducked behind his cushion shield and froze.

The kitchen table began to buck and leap. It smashed itself repeatedly against the doorway into the hall until its legs broke off and it spun into the understairs cupboard with a deafening crash. All the funny toys scuttled out of sight. One by one, lightbulbs shattered throughout the house and the TV turned itself off. The living room was dark except for the orangey glow of street lights through the patterned curtains. Howling sounds circled above. William shrunk into himself. Anguished, seething screams flew from room to room. The entire house seemed to shiver.

The goblin was furious. It hadn't had a tantrum like this since its pets had first been taught the rules. Their quiet routine had kept it calm, and amused.

Didn't want stupid pets anyway! Bored of them. Spoiled now. Not a complete set any more. Broken.

The howls distorted, fading into the darkness. For a long time, nobody moved or spoke. Mum's hands were flat to her head, pressing back her hair. It felt to William as if the slightest sound or motion would change the world.

The door to the kitchen was wide open. Grey shapes and shadows were visible, familiar outlines.

Something else was visible too. A shadow which didn't correspond to any object in there. William thought it might be the wrecked table but, no, that was out in the hall, and it had straight edges, not curved.

Was this conjured by the goblin? Was it a new toy?

William pressed the lower half of his face into his shield, his eyes wide and fixed on the doorway (one, two, three, four, three, two, one, repeat). The shadow was the darkest of darks, a shadow in a room with no light to cast it. Not a toy. His brain seemed to throb with certainty.

It was the goblin itself in the kitchen. The goblin none of them had ever seen, for real. It had crept out of the walls, slid from under the wallpaper.

The shadow moved. Shadow claws hooked and sharpened. Shadow body, humped, twisted. What could make a shadow like that?

William watched in a daze, quick breath hot and wet against the cushion. Mum jumped to her feet and ran into the kitchen. Paul shouted something. Mum shouted something back, then her scream of terror was cut short. Broken. Like Dad, but deliberately. And magicked away. Paul shouted and shouted. He picked up the little coffee table and raced after Mum, holding it above his head as a weapon. He shrieked. Gone.

Get rid of the lot. Don't want these pets. No fun now. Spoiled.

A shifting of shapes sent William scrambling. He tumbled off the sofa and ran, taking care to skip over all the bits of shattered lightbulb. He climbed the stairs two at a time and stopped at the top. He didn't know what to do.

Hide. Hide from the goblin. Perhaps, if he was good, it would go away? Perhaps, if he was very quiet, and didn't cry or anything, it would leave him alone? The funny toys hurt him less when he didn't bawl or fight them off, so this should be the same, right? Do as normal. Do the same as always.

Shakily, he brushed his teeth and put on his jarmies. He looked at his calendar, Monday 9th October, and crossed it off with his stubby pencil. Another day done. He got into bed, but didn't read a chapter of his current book because the light was smashed and it was too dark to see. He pulled the sheets up to his chin.

From downstairs came the soft crunch of trodden glass.

He shut his eyes and made his nightly wish. Please, please, let me sleep and never wake.

Crunch.

He didn't want to die, he wanted peace, that was all. He wanted everything to stop, cease, halt.

The creak of a footstep at the bottom of the stairs. And then another.

He wished, wished, wished for time to stop. Stop now. And stop now. Didn't matter about the dark, that was OK, stop now.

Creak. Creak. Creak.

Please.

Creak. Creak. Creak.

He wished for sleep eternal, for existence in dreams, for an end to this life.

The turning of the handle on his door.

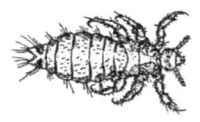

Boneweed smiled slyly to himself. He held the fixed attentions of his listeners, the royal household and their high hallthanes. The aches in their bones were growing, but the fog of bewitchment calmed all misgivings. Their faces were bright and rosy and well-defined, as if colourfully painted onto smooth heads.

"Might I enquire," said Boneweed, sliding a manuscript from a drawer on his cart, "why the court's resident wishfellow is not present at this evening's entertainment?"

Despite themselves, every courtier in the ballroom took a sharp inward breath! All eyes snapped to the king and queen.

Croaknot took a step. "The Djinn Of Continuum is not so permitted," he said with absolute finality.

"My humblest apologies," said Boneweed. "I travelled once in the verdant fragrance of the North Shores, where the Djinn Of Flora may be freely consulted. I was forgetting the vastly more dangerous power of Their Majesties' own spellhurler. Curiosity stole my tongue."

"It did," said Croaknot flatly.

The king and queen were eyeing the manuscript in Boneweed's hands. His sly smile broadened a little. The fact that his head was still attached to his body was proof that his plan was working.

Regime Change
part 2: the dinner party

I'm in my office, on the top floor at the campus. It's getting colder outside, I can see flecks of frost clinging to the grass at the borders of the car park down there, and there's a moustache of condensation along the bottom of my window. The silence, in this moment, is so profound it feels as if the world has ended, as if the entire storm of life has paused.

I've been feeling low for some time. Helpless and grey. But I'm better now, I really am. Sometimes, it feels as if everything is speeding up, unstoppably, a dream in which the seconds are ticking faster and faster, demanding I decide, decide, decide. Sometimes, the weight of everything is like Fuseli's nightmare incubus crushing the air from my lungs, like a giant block of stone grinding me to dust. Sometimes, everything feels so fragile it dissolves in a breath of air. It's so easy to sink, but I've learned how to float, I've regained my balance and I'm quietly proud of myself for that.

My awakening to Truth has helped me find a fresh perspective. Visits from the little people, late at night, have taught me what to expect. There's to be regime change in the world, very soon. A change of ownership. New management. The demon heralds arrived in this world a while ago and have been spreading the good news. It's hard to avoid a sense of excitement but, until the trumpet sounds, everyone must remain absolutely as normal. The unfaithful must not suspect, shhhh!

The phone in the outer office suddenly rings. Nobody's picking up so I answer it myself. "Sociology department, Amy

Gledhill speaking... Oh Hettie, hi!... No, no, I'm sitting here marking essays and staring out of the window. How are you?... Really? Oh, that's wonderful!... Congratulations, I'm so happy for you... Yes... It is, yes... How's Pete taking it...?" I laugh, my fingers pressed to my face. "Is he?... Aw, bless... Listen, I was going to call you anyway. How do you fancy an old-fashioned suburban dinner party?... Yeah, very!" I laugh again. "Yes, at mine? Week on Friday at eight?... Brilliant... Well, definitely, the countdown to big life changes has begin, so make the most of it, eh?... Oh, only half a dozen... I thought I'd invite my colleague Len and his wife, they lived in the Far East like you and Pete, you can compare notes... Japan and Korea, mostly... Yeah... Yeah!... And my brother Alfie's back living with me again, so he'll be there... No, completely base over apex, unfortunately... Yes, very badly, I'm afraid, it was a terrible blow... But then he's a FUCKING BRAIN-DEAD WEASEL SHIT STAIN WITH A FAT CUNT GIRLFRIEND, so I'm past caring, really... Sorry?... Yes, I'm fine, why?... I said what?... Did I?... No, I'm fine, honestly, if anything my day's been a bit slow... Oh, yes, of course, you've got a whole list to call with your news, sorry... See you next Friday, then?... Lovely, bye."

So nice to hear from her! We were at uni together. She and her husband have just moved house a five minute drive from me, so we'll see each other more often from now on.

Tick.

Tock.

Next Friday.

"What's that?" says Val, Len Kendrick's wife. "Did you hear something outside? Like a sort of howling? In the distance?" Her words are slightly slurred.

I'm suddenly glowing with excitement and merriment. That was the trumpet call! The clarion cry of the wild hunt, the celebration, the arrival of His new world! I *knew* it would come tonight, I felt it in my bones. I felt it on my skin. I have worn my best dress, had my hair done specially for the occasion, applied my favourite lippy.

"I didn't hear it," says Gemma-Louise. Of course you didn't hear it, lard-arse, you were too busy wiping the last smear of sauce off your plate with a bit of bread. Gemma-Louise is Alfie's circular girlfriend from the flats over the road. Too dim and lazy to find love outside their own postcode, both of them.

Neither Alfie nor Len hear the trumpet call either. Alfie's telling stupid jokes and Len's trying to focus on his wine glass.

It's a shame Hettie and Pete haven't made it to tonight's dinner party. No call, no text. Rude. I hope they're IN A DITCH, GUSHING BLOOD.

Meanwhile, ladies and gentlemen, the evening has gone really well so far:

STARTER – stuffed mushrooms

I pretend I've made them myself. I squish them about a bit with my thumb, so they look more home-done. I delay and delay serving because ooooh I could feel that trumpet call a-comin' and I want to be ready when the fun begins. I keep saying we'll hang on a bit, in case Hettie and Pete are running late, then when that excuse wears thin I claim I'm solving a minor problem in the kitchen.

MAIN COURSE – lasagne

In the end, I went for a simple pasta dish after all. After a lot of cookery show watching and recipe book reading, I *had* been planning to do something a little daring, steamed sea bass with spiced herb gnocchi, slow-cooked onions and a horseradish sauce, but I couldn't be arsed.

I delay and delay, to get them all nice and pissed. They stay in their seats, yakking and swigging and hungry, laughing and drinking and trying not to nibble too much garlic bread or it might spoil their appetite.

Everyone tucks in heartily when it finally appears. Pigs at a fucking trough.

Oh dammit! I missed a trick! I could have put something in the lasagne, something chemical, mixed it in. They'd never have noticed. Aww.

They sit at the table, the cloth strewn with flecks of cheese sauce and empty bottles and little splashes of wine. I clear away their plates while they chatter.

Tonight, I've put up both the fold-up wings on the dining table. This way, it takes up half the room but there's plenty of space for everyone and the white Dunelm tablecloth is big enough. Len and Val – neat, academic, youthfully middle-aged, don't go out much in the evenings – are next to each other on the side nearest the stairs, Alfie opposite, all T-shirt and teeth, me next to Alfie, Emma-Louise at one end because if you put her beside pipe cleaner Alfie their shapes will make the number 10 in human form and I don't want distractions. Not on this special night.

The lighting is subtle, two lamps plus a battery candle-effect thing centrepiece for the table. A selection of 1990s hits plays softly from the Bluetooth speaker on the bookshelves.

DESSERT – assorted nasty deaths

Now it's one whole minute since the call to arms. Come on, I tell myself, no dawdling, it's time to begin! I think of all the games that will be being played, down the street, through the town, along the motorways. In here, the sound from outside has been forgotten.

"Hey, hey," says Alfie. "I'm on a whiskey diet."

"A whiskey diet?" says Len, genuinely puzzled. He's a joke teller's dream come true.

"Yeah, I've lost three days already."

Len laughs so hard he starts wheezing. He's been drinking to offset Alfie's boorishness and my deliberate delays, and now he's sozzled enough to find Alfie a wonderful evening's entertainment. Gemma-Louise snorts with mirth and nods at Len, amused by his amusement.

"I was asked, do you always drink whisky neat?" says Alfie. "I said, no, sometimes I drink in my pants."

Even Val giggles at that one, which is a relief because her resting bitch face looks like an angry pug in a bowl of lemon juice. You feeling a bit icky, Val? You look a bit icky. That'll be the bottle and a half of red you've necked.

Len dabs his eyes. "Oh dear oh dear. I'm so glad we don't have to be up in the morning, I think I might have had a tiny bit too much of that excellent scotch of yours, Alfie, so… I'll have one more please."

He and Alfie laugh and Alfie pours him one more please of the twelve-year-old single malt I bought. With my money.

"I think I've had too much too," says Val quietly. Nobody else is listening.

Len says to Gemma-Louise "You don't have to be up in the morning, do you?"

"No, thank fuck," says Gemma-Louise. "I would have been at work tonight, but I managed to get today and tomorrow off."

"Where is it you work?" says Len.

"The petrol station shop, y'know, by the junction?"

"Ooh, yes?" says Len, as if she'd said she's personal assistant to a Arab prince. "Yes, I think I know it."

"OK, OK," says Alfie, "there's an axe murderer and a young girl, and they're walking through a dark forest, right? Right?" Don't worry, Alfie, we're hanging off your every word. "And the girl says it's getting really dark around here and I'm getting really scared. And then the axe murderer says what, *you're* scared? I've got to walk home all by myself."

I don't get it for a moment or two. I must have had a bit too much as well. Len covers his face with a hand and cackles. "Where do you get all these from?"

Val's getting a funny look on her face. Well, funn*ier.* She's going a little bit green.

"Come on, Val," I say, hopping over to her side of the table, "I can see the warning signs, I'll be your hair-holder-back for this evening."

"You all right, dear?" mutters Len.

She nods and frowns. It's the loss of dignity she minds, not the greedy intake of alcohol. I put my arm across her shoulders and guide her to the stairs. What she's wearing is rather too sparkly for the occasion, but honestly Val it's great the vintage stuff you can find in the charity shops these days.

Alfie scratches at his faux-intellectual goatee. "Aaah, I've got a great one. Wait a minute, got to remember it all, it's a long one…" Len and Gemma-Louise are all agog. Val and I make our way up the stairs, Alfie's braying voice following close behind.

He puts his little finger and thumb to his ear to indicate a telephone. "OK, I'm an answer machine, right, yeh?" Len and Gemma-Louise chuckle. "Good evening, thank you for calling the mental health hotline. Please choose one of the following options. If you are obsessive-compulsive, please press One… thirty-seven times…"

Len and Gemma-Louise variously howl, snort and guffaw almost continuously as Alfie carries on. "If…" he almost can't speak for smirking. "If you have anxiety issues, please ask someone to press Two for you…"

At the top of the stairs, I don't bother to turn the light on. I steer Val into the bathroom. I can see she's concentrating hard on not vomiting before her hands touch porcelain.

"If you have… oh, how does it--? Oh yeh, if you suffer from multiple personalities, please press Three, Four, Five and Six..."

Val delicately drops to her knees in front of the toilet. I think she wants to wave me away, but I expect the room's spinning quite fast and she needs to put all her effort into staying vertical and clutching the sides. She bends forward and heaves, heavily spattering the bowl.

Here comes the fun.

"If you are paranoid, stay on the line while we trace this call…" Len and Gemma-Louise are honking like sea lions.

I stand, put a hand around the back of Val's head and a knee against her back. I press down with my full weight.

"If you are experiencing hallucinations, the clown standing beside you will tell you which number to press…"

Val struggles wildly. She's surprisingly lively, but I have a firm grip of her. Her face is well under the water and the noises she makes are – if you'll pardon the pun – drowned out by the raucous laughter from downstairs.

"If you have severe memory loss, please press Seven and state your name, address, phone number, first pet's name, date of birth, National Insurance number and mother's maiden name…"

Val bucks weakly for a few more seconds, then her muscles slacken. I take my hand away and she stays wedged, head down. Blimey, I don't know me own strength, me!

"If you are suffering from low self-esteem, please hang up, we don't want to talk to you..."

I notice there are some splashes of sick on my hand and I shudder. Disgusted, I wash them off using plenty of soap, then I go downstairs.

"If you have amnesia, please press Eight... If you have amnesia, please press Eight... If you have amnesia, please press Eight..."

Once the laughter has subsided, Len says to me "Is Val OK?"

"Oh, yes, fine," I reassure him. "She's just having a bit of a lie down."

"Ah, that's a relief," says Len. "Er, I think I'll call a cab in ten minutes, if that's all right. I can't believe what the time is, we mustn't outstay our welcome."

"There's no chance of that, Len," I smile.

"Last one, then, last one," says Alfie. "OK, what's got two legs and bleeds all over the place?"

"I don'know," says Gemma-Louise through a fog of booze, "what's got two legs and bleeds all over the place?"

"Half a cat," says Alfie.

"Eurrggh!"

My turn. "Tell you what," I say, "before we call it a night, I've got a great game we can play."

"We're not starting on your boooooored games!" says Alfie.

"No, definitely not," I say, "this is totally different." I go to the little cupboard under the bookshelves and take out a ball of jute garden string.

"Oh no, not the stupid game with the key ring," moans Alfie.

"Is it the Indian rope trick done with mice?" says Len. Nobody laughs.

"No, and no," I say. "Sit upright in your chairs." They're too drunk to think this is anything weird, they play along. Hee hee.

I quickly wind the string around them and their chairs, around and around and around, nice and tight.

"What's the game?" says Alfie. "Have we got to pick something up with our teeth? It better not be anything disgusting!"

"It's an escapology act!" pipes up Len. "Ah, no, we're the ones tied up."

All three of them are fixed in place, arms and legs and torsos in a wild net of string. I clamber up onto the dining table and kick off all the plates and other crap. It all bumps and crashes onto the floor.

"Watch out for red wine stains!" cries Len. Now the three of them laugh, more out of nerves than amusement. They sense something isn't quite right here. Ha ha.

I stand on the table. My hair brushes the ceiling. I place one high heel against Len's chest and give him a sharp push. His chair tips back and thumps against the wall behind at a sharp angle. The tangle of string criss-crossing the room pulls the other two chairs a bit closer. Len cries out as he falls, thinking he's going to smack the back of his head.

"What the fuck--?" shouts Alfie.

"Amy, what are you doing?" shouts Gemma-Louise at the same time.

I pounce on Len. Like a beast. Like a predator.

His face swims with fear. He's sobered up all of a sudden.

"W-What the devil--?" he stammers.

"Question one!" I cry, my face close to his. "Your category is Ancient Mythology. What do Tiresias the prophet, Justitia the goddess, and the Norse god Höðr all have in common? C'mon, c'mon, tick tock."

He looks at me, his eyes filled with confusion and disbelief. He's so confused, the silly old fool actually gives me the answer. "Y-You mean, that they were blind?"

"Bong!" I cry. "Correct! They were, indeed, all blind!"

Even thick-as-shit Alfie and Gemma-Louise see where this is going before Len does. They start shouting and struggling. Softly, in the background, those '90s hits carry on a-popping and a-bopping.

I stab a finger into Len's left eye. He screams and wriggles. I hook it out and it ss-plops as it pulls free. With a jerk, I snap the optic nerve.

I tell you, Alfie and Gemma-Louise are going *mental*. They're bouncing up and down, trying to shift their chairs or break free, it's *hilarious*. Gemma-Louise is bright red in the face, her blubber's wobbling, I think to myself I'm glad this is a concrete floor. Len's face is an absolute picture.

I kick off my shoes and stand beside Len's chair. He's shaking like a leaf. I use thumb and middle finger on the other eye. I toss it over my shoulder. Blood wells up all over Len's face. It dribbles into his gaping mouth. He stops shivering. Shit, I think he's died of shock. Not fair.

"Fuck you! Fuck this! Lemme go!" yells Alfie. "*Help! Help!*"

Gemma-Louise joins in. I cup a hand behind my ear and stare at her until she realises she's wasting her breath. The little she has left.

She babbles at me. "Please don't please don't please, I've done nothing wrong I'm a good person, please don't blind me please don't do this."

"Ohhh, lumpy," I pout, gently patting her big, doughy cheek, "I'm not going to blind you. I'm not, honest."

She pauses mid-sentence, sweat shining her face and neck. Alfie just sort of gibbers, in between telling me to fuck myself and straining to break his bonds. No point, you snivelling waste of skin, that string has one hell of a breaking strain. I checked.

"Fuck you! Fuck you!" he yells.

"Question *two*!" I cry, sticking two fingers up at Gemma-Louise. "The category is Science. How much energy is released by the breakdown of one cubic centimetre of human fat? Here's a clue, the energy can be derived in the form of heat."

"What?" screeches Gemma-Louise. "I don't fucking know! What the fuck's that supposed to mean?"

"B'up-errrr," I say. "Incorrect. To find the correct answer, let's conduct an experiment."

I fetch the twelve-year-old single malt. There's about half the bottle left. For a moment, from the look on her face, Gemma-Louise thinks I'm going to make her drink it all. Daft bitch. I turn the bottle upside down and pour the whiskey all over her. I toss the bottle aside and hop back onto the dining table, stepping away from her a little.

They both fall silent, her and Alfie. I smile at them. Slowly, I reach behind the waistband of my dress and pull out what I've had hidden there for hours. It's… a… box of matches!

They start to squirm and scream again. Carefully, with a theatrical flourish, I open the box and take out a match. Schikk! It's alight!

"Noooo! NOOOO! NOOOOOO!"

"Put it down! Put it down! I'll fucking *kill you*!"

I flick the match. It spins through the air and lands – perfection! – on Gemma-Louise at the *precise* point between her shimmering breasts.

The flames are so huge and hot I have to shield my face with a hand, the heat coming off her really is quite extraordinary, and the sound she's making is somewhere up in the hearing range of dogs. Alfie, England's premier useless turd, just sets his face into this ugly great gaping screech.

A grey shroud of smoke is quickly gathering around the ceiling. Good thing I remembered to take the batteries out of the smoke alarms!

Alfie's lips judder as he tries to speak. "W-Why?… Why?"

"Why?" I say. "Because the hunt has begun. The faithful are rising up! We're making a new world, now, tonight, and forever, free from ghastly little shits like you. A new world, for the strong and resourceful."

His eyes begin to leak, his lips to wobble. "W-What are you going to do to me?"

I lean as close to him as the flames of his burning girlfriend will allow. "Question three. Etymology."

"What th—?"

"What is the dictionary definition of the word anthropophagus?"

He stares rigidly at me. "What are you going to do?" he sobs.

I shake my head slowly, my lips pursed with regret. "Oooh dear, sorry, that's not the answer I was looking for. I'll give you a clue, there's likely to be a lot of them about this evening, roaming the area, and I'm going to leave you here, trussed up and ready for them."

Even in the light from his burning friend, which is less intense now she's lost so much weight (hey, well done, you!) I can see he's going pale.

"Not even a guess?" I coax. "I'm afraid that means zero points on the word knowledge round, anthropophagus is another word for cannibal, a human being who eats the flesh of other human beings. Well, so long, and thanks for playing!"

I skip away, dancing to the tune of his pleas, admiring my own cleverness. I run out of the house, into the dark night and down our road, where screams and laughter rise behind firmly closed curtains. The streets are beginning to fill, runners and hiders, chasers and cutters, brutes and beasts. On the horizon, there is the rouge of firelight. I join the hunt.

The ballroom braziers spat and crackled, and the storm hammered the night, but everyone who was gathered to hear tales from Boneweed's library was becoming unnaturally still, unnaturally silent. They felt the pull of the wordweave, its delicate twine binding their minds like the siren call of songfish across the sea. They felt strange changes inside themselves.

With a mischievous giggle, Boneweed hot-stepped to his cart, carefully put away one manuscript and fetched out another.

The Diary Of
Edward Albert Towns

I have kept a diary, in one form or another – sometimes sketchy, sometimes at length – for the better part of twenty-five years. Indeed, for the majority of my life. But I find myself, today, unable to comprehend the true nature of that life or the many pages upon which its events have been recorded. I cannot even begin this entry with the date.

I do not know when I am. I know *where*, at least I think I do, but I'm still not sure when. My hope at this moment is that in setting down the peculiar hours which have just passed, I may at least clarify my nightmarish thoughts. Writing my diary has always allowed me to gain fresh perspective and to approach problems with greater objectivity.

It was at eight o'clock yesterday, the evening of Wednesday 27th January 1850 – of that I am certain! – when Agatha and I alighted from her father's carriage in Norton Place and presented ourselves at the home of her friend Mrs Dyall. The evening was a dark and choking one, the air filled with soot smuts as big as snowflakes. A foulness arose from the effluvia of the streets which was noxious enough to have us both holding handkerchiefs to our faces. As we walked, I hovered a protective arm around Agatha's shoulders, as if this might spare her shoes from staining!

The Dyalls' town house is a grand one, a four-storey residence situated half way along a curving terrace of similar dwellings. Unlike some of its immediate neighbours, its windows were filled with the warm, homely glow of candlelight, a sign of the activity within.

No sooner were we in the vestibule than a pleasant babble of convivial voices rushed to greet us, as did Mrs Dyall, her arms outstretched towards Agatha and the grin on her face surely a mile wide. She and my beloved have been boon companions for many years, their intimacy a testament to the old maxim that virtue finds a mirror of itself in friendships.

Mr Dyall, a printer by trade, is of an equally gregarious nature and although my acquaintance with him spans only the few months since my engagement to Agatha, I already consider him a trusted associate. When we were shown into the drawing room he weaved his way around the other guests to welcome us.

Over sherry and seed cake, he proved to be in a teasing mood. "Is the wedding date decided?" he said, with eyebrows raised and bald head gleaming.

Agatha and I exchanged glances. "Not yet," I confessed with a smile. "Not quite."

"Oh, Towns," he said, pulling his face tight in comic exaggeration, "you risk disaster! Disaster, I tell you! A girl of such rare quality might at any moment be lured away by the jingling gold of some fiendish mill owner!"

His wife let fly a cry of derision and leaned closer to him. "Oh, if only we lived in an industrial district, think what I might have been spared!" It took poor Dyall a moment or two to catch up with our merriment.

The drawing room was one I had not had occasion to visit before, a large and tastefully decorated salon with a heartily blazing fireplace and thoughtfully arranged candelabras which gave the scene an atmosphere of cosy domesticity. There were nine or ten other guests present, including Mr Dyall's parents, a most engaging couple down from Staffordshire.

The main aim of the evening being musical, we all took seats while Mrs Dyall's sister Elizabeth arranged herself at the keys of an antique harpsichord, its sides elaborately painted with grape vines. Miss Elizabeth's playing was beautiful, despite an occasional hesitancy, and we were entertained with a variety of traditional melodies.

Once or twice, as delicate notes swirled around us, I happened to glance across at Agatha. Each time I did so, I felt a fresh glow of admiration and love for her. She is exquisite. My heart is hers alone.

When the recital was done, Miss Elizabeth's blushes at the guests' appreciation were like scarlet roses on her cheeks. Hereupon Mr Dyall, to much laughter, announced that his noodlings on the violin would begin shortly, and thus sensitive persons were warned to leave the premises with all due haste.

It was during this intermezzo, when the general chit-chat resumed, we became party to a conversation between Mr Dyall and a hawkish, rather saturnine gentleman of bountiful tailoring called Clements. "Oh, since infancy," Dyall was saying airily, patting his shiny cranium, "every lotion and potion on the market has been applied to this dome of mine at one time or other, to no avail. I'm simply inured to it now, happy to be of rare convenience to any bump-reading phrenologists I happen to encounter."

Clements remained stony-faced. "Has mesmeric treatment been tried?" he asked, his voice deep and resonant. "I'm unaware of any previous use specific to hair loss, but mesmerism's physiological effects are both wide-ranging and proven."

At this point Mr Dyall Senior, who is a retired physician, stepped in to denounce Clements's assertion with considerable vigour. "Mesmerism is quackery," he expostulated. "Only a fool would think otherwise. It has no basis in fact and no place in modern medical practice."

"On the contrary, Sir," said Clements, his countenance darkening, "mesmeric techniques are fully documented for the curing of seizures, neuralgia, dyspepsia, lethargy, melancholia, hysterical symptoms of many kinds and *all* forms of pain, both chronic and transient. Patients have for many years benefitted from mesmerism in body and mind, despite the blind prejudices of misinformed sawbones."

"I have never witnessed any such benefits," said Dyall Snr., puffing out his chest in indignation, "but I did once witness one of Elliotson's notorious trance sessions, and a more contemptible exhibition of cheap theatrical fakery it is impossible to imagine!"

"Let me inform you, Sir," growled Clements, "I studied under both Dr Ellliotson and the Baron Dupotet himself."

Their discourse, having assumed an angry aspect, was cut short by our hostess Mrs Dyall, who brightly suggested a way to determine the reality of mesmeric influence, namely a brief demonstration ahead of her husband's imminent violin tomfoolery. Clements muttered something about triviality but agreed, if Mrs Dyall would consent to being his subject. She subtly glared her grumbling father-in-law into submission.

The guests gathered around in excited curiosity, one or two of them commenting on the evening's delightful capriciousness. Clements equipped himself with a candle and an empty crystal goblet, and placed three chairs side by side before the fireplace. Seating himself on a fourth, facing them, he asked Mrs Dyall to sit in the middle chair of the three. Here, facing Clements, their knees were almost touching.

Clements held up the goblet with the candle behind it, turning the glass such that light glittered across Mrs Dyall's face. "Listen to my voice," he said softly. "Watch the light in the glass." He continued to speak in a low, even tone, Mrs Dyall staring ever more fixedly ahead. After a minute or more, during which no guest dared draw breath, her eyelids began to droop.

"You are asleep now," said Clements. "You are aware of nothing but my voice." He turned to the onlookers. "In a trance state, the patient cannot feel pain." He unhooked a tie pin from his throat. "Hold out your hand please, Mrs Dyall." She did so, and he lightly jabbed the sharp end of the pin into her palm!

She did not so much as wince. A subdued murmur of astonishment went through the room. To show this was not an isolated effect, Clements made a second jab, this time with greater force, at the flesh around her thumb. Again, there was no reaction whatsoever.

"Please lie down across the chairs." Mrs Dyall obeyed, head and shoulders resting on one chair, lower torso on the next, feet on the last.

Clements moved to stand behind the middle chair. "The patient's musculature is under her complete control." Carefully, he slid the middle chair away, leaving Mrs Dyall like a plank of wood, held up only at her extremities.

Then, to the absolute amazement of all present, he took away the first chair too! Her head remained motionless! "Not trickery," said Clements, firmly, "but absolute control originating in the calves and ankles."

He replaced the chairs and bid Mrs Dyall to sit upright again. Upon his placing of a finger on her forehead she suddenly regained her waking state and duly declared what a peaceful sleep she'd had.

The hubbub which followed was extraordinary. Mr Dyall Snr looked utterly dumbfounded. His son, ready with violin, simply put the instrument back in its case. Mr Clements evinced no pleasure in his remarkable feat, but instead asked for permission to show his skill in mesmerism in its proper medical context. "Does anyone here," he said, "suffer from regular pains in the legs? Or a nervous trembling of the hands, perhaps? I can promise immediate relief."

Agatha kept pressing me in the ribs, urging me to ask whether Clements might alleviate the debilitating headaches which have plagued me for so long. After some reluctance, I put myself forward.

I wish to almighty God I had not. I wish I had run from the room, from the entire house.

Clements sat me down opposite him, exactly in the manner of Mrs Dyall. I looked into his dark eyes. The illuminated goblet rose into view.

"Watch the lights in the glass."

I did so. The goblet seemed to be spinning before my eyes. Points of light, like stars in the night sky, twinkled in complex patterns through the finely cut facets of the glass. Regular and pulsing. I forgot the drawing room. I was alone in silence, peaceful silence, warming silence, tender silence, and—

—I gasped sharply, as if suddenly remembering to breathe. My eyes snapped open on a cluttered, fusty little study filled with creaking bookshelves and worn out wooden furniture. It was broad daylight. Hot streaks of sunshine lanced through rickety windows, shining on a billion slowly churning motes of dust. Outside, trees swayed slowly.

I was resting against a bank of large cushions on a frayed and overstuffed chaise. I was wearing an oddly styled suit made from thick cloth in a vaguely herringbone pattern.

A man's face suddenly loomed in front of me. "How are you, old man? Are you with us, Farley?" He was chubby, with short fair hair and a moustache like a mighty caterpillar.

"Where am I?" I muttered.

The face twiddled in thought for a moment. A hand appeared and snapped fingers at me a couple of times. "Don't worry, I expect the effects will wear off in a moment or two."

"Effects?" I mumbled, my mouth feeling as dry as a desert. "Of the mesmerism? The trance?"

"That's it," grinned the face. "You didn't say a word while you were under, unfortunately. Back in the land of the living now, though."

The face retreated and I saw it belonged to an overweight young man dressed almost identically to me apart from a pair of shiny black riding boots. As he dropped back into an old armchair, I noticed for the first time that there were two others, perched at either end of a settee beside an overflowing roll-top bureau. One was a man with a greying beard, some years older than I, his bony hands clasped to a peak over the top of a walking cane. The other was a young woman wearing round spectacles, a stern expression, and a dress I took to be of foreign fashion since it was oddly slender in shape.

My feelings of intense confusion must have been all too visible on my face. All three of them regarded me with an air of guarded disappointment.

"You did visit the spirit world?" said the young man.

"Were you in contact with the dead?" said the older man, in a strong Eastern Euopean accent.

I found my hands pressed to my temples. "The dead?" I whispered, cold fear rising up my spine. "I don't understand."

"I told you," the young woman declared to her colleagues with finality. "I told you it wouldn't work. You're supposed to darken the room and sit around a table holding hands. I've seen it done. You'll never get results if you carry on being slapdash about it."

"Where am I?" I repeated, my fear beginning to transmute into nervous agitation. "Who are you?"

"There, you see?" said the woman. "All you've accomplished is to put poor Mr Farley into a complete funk."

"My name is not Farley," I said. "It is Towns. Edward Towns. I demand to know where I am and what has happened to me!"

"You think your name is Towns?" said the young man.

"I don't *think* my name is Towns," I cried, "it *is* Towns! And has been for my entire life!"

"I say, this is fascinating," breathed the young man, edging forward on his seat. "No, Miss Searle, I think it worked after all."

The older man edged closer too. "Our friend's mediumship must be, as he suspected, of extraordinary sensitivity," he said, plucking at his lower lip. "To have made a bond which transcends the hypnotic state. Or, could it be, he is still in his hypnotic state? Might this be his communion with the spirits, a communion which simply took a while to establish?"

My nerves were now ragged in the extreme, but the older man's words sparked a little rationality in my thoughts. I pressed myself into the bank of cushions behind me, shakily rubbing a hand at my forehead.

"Yes, that could be it," I muttered to myself. "*This* is an illusion, brought on by the mesmeric unconsciousness into which Mr Clements has placed me. I am sleeping, hallucinating, imagining."

The three strangers looked at me as if I were some breed of talking monkey! "Contact or not," said the woman, this Miss Searle, peering over her spectacles, "his mind is clearly stuck fast! I knew no good would come of this. We dabble with mystic forces at our peril."

They continued to discuss me. I attempted to ignore them. I closed my eyes, breathed deeply, and waited for Clements to awaken me. Of all the absurd delusions…! What was keeping the man?

When, eventually, after many minutes had passed and nothing had changed, I began to feel agitated again. Mrs Dyall hadn't emerged from some peculiar fiction – a restful sleep, she'd said! – so why was *I* having to endure one? By the ticking clock on the mantelpiece almost a half hour had now passed since my 'arrival' here.

A half hour… of dreaming? Moreover, dreaming with such un-dream-like solidity and in such un-dream-like detail as to be indistinguishable from hard reality. Was such a thing to be expected in a mesmeric trance? How the devil was this supposed to be curing my headaches? A half hour of dreaming in which I could pinch the back of my hand, feel the warmth of sunlight, dream up a place I'd never been and people I had never met?

Suddenly, an icy horror coursed through my veins. I interrupted the strangers' deliberations. "Are you implying that I am the *ghost* of Edward Towns, now resident in the body of someone named Farley? That I died in the Dyalls' drawing room in January and have now reincarnated, displacing Farley forever?"

"No. No, no, good heavens, no," said the younger man, scratching at his moustache. "I don't think that's it at all, old chap. Never heard of anything quite so curious! Have you, Karvitch? Miss Searle?"

"Never," they replied, evidently nonplussed.

I took the opportunity to stand, pick up a framed photograph, and angle it to the window so my reflection was visible in its glass surface. The face I saw was my own, perfectly familiar, albeit with a rather more cropped hairstyle than hitherto. I was no ghost. Replacing the picture, I returned to the chaise.

"I think," said the younger man, patting a thick book which rested on the arm of his chair, "when I put the 'fluence on you, it conked you out as described in chapter seven but didn't go the whole way, perhaps due to the amateur slapdashery Miss Searle has mentioned. You were unconscious, but didn't connect with the spirit realm, and so your mind concocted a whole new world for yourself. To fill the gap, as it were. Remember, this is one of the dead ends it warns about in chapter three. Miss Searle is quite right, we shouldn't have let our enthusiasm for spiritualist investigation run away with us. My fault entirely, old chap, no china shop is safe with a bull like me around, eh?"

"But—" I stammered, thoroughly unnerved at this suggestion. "For how long was I insensible?"

"Oh, I'd say, twenty minutes?"

"And in twenty minutes I lived more than thirty years of an entirely different life?" I said, aghast.

"I expect much of it was assumed to exist? To account for where you thought you were at the time? What makes you think *that* life was real and *this* one isn't?"

"Because… I remember it!" I cried.

"As clearly as you see us now?" he said, "Or this room? Or those trees out there? I assure you, it'll all fade away soon and you'll recall who you really are." He tapped the book's cover. "It's all in here. You've read it yourself."

"I have not," I said through gritted teeth. "I knew nothing about mesmerism until this eve—" I found my hands tightening into fists. "I certainly don't remember either your face or your name."

"Harris," he said brightly. "We read at Oxford together. Don't worry, it'll come back. I tell you what, to help it along, describe Edward Towns to us. His life, what you were doing before you woke up."

"*My* life."

Harris nodded indulgently. "As you say."

It seemed a reasonable way to order my thoughts, so I related an outline of my boyhood, my education, my career, and the events – including my engagement to Agatha – leading up to the *soirée* at Norton Place. It was quickly evident that the ease of my recollections and the detail in which I could answer their questions impressed all three of them. *They* seemed as astonished at my certainty and erudition as *I* was to be sitting there in front of them!

"It all fits," said Harris at last, eyes narrowing and head nodding. "Much of what you've told us chimes closely with your own life— er, with the life of Herbert Farley, I should say. Very similar background, very similar upbringing, very similar everything, pretty much. Your mind found itself adrift, being in a trance, and so it weaved lots of personal details into a bit of biographical make-believe. Think about it: how did you exit this make-believe? Through. Being. Mesmerised. Now, that makes sense, does it not? Ah, and here's proof positive that it was all in your head, the floating lady, Mrs

Whatdyoucallher, suspended on her ankles in mid-air. An occurrence plainly impossible in real life, but mere everyday this 'n' that when it turns up in a dream. You know, that might have been your brain giving you a bit of a reminder, don't you think? A sort of clue."

The older man, Karvitch, rocked side to side, his cane like the arm of a metronome and his features mobile with indecision. "I am still inclined towards the displacement theory," he mused.

"Let's hope to goodness you're wrong," said Miss Searle, "otherwise Mr Farley might be helplessly trapped in this body, unable to regain control."

"Or moved to another plane of existence entirely," said Karvitch.

Harris held up both palms. "Ah, no, let's not jump to conclusions. Farley will be himself again in no time, I'm sure, the old noggin's just shaken up for the time being." He looked at me with an expression like a puppy expecting a walk.

I felt a rush of indignation. "But what about Agatha?" I said, my voice suddenly sharper than I had intended. "Where is my fiancé? If, as you claim, my life here finds many echoes in that of Edward Towns, then where is *her* echo?"

"I'm afraid we don't know any Agathas," said Harris. "And you have no fiancé, you're very much the confirmed bachelor, I'm afraid."

This bitter revelation was more than I could stand. To be expected to abandon my history was torment in itself, but to abandon the love of my life was utterly beyond endurance! How could she possibly be a phantom of my own devising? We had met, unexpectedly, we had grown to know, then like, then love one another, she had surprised me constantly, delighted me in a hundred different ways because her nature was so different to my own. To be with her was to be improved in my own character! To suggest that she was lost in the mists of a dream – that, indeed, she had never existed at all! – was insulting and absurd. My love for her was real and true. I could not and would not accept her absence!

After some minutes, I announced that I wished to be alone with my thoughts and could no longer bear company. The three of them murmured complete understanding, Harris expressing again his certainty that I would be as right as rain after a good sleep in my own bed.

It was as I rose to leave that I saw the newspaper folded on top of the bureau. I picked it up with trembling fingers. Here, at least, was an answer to my question about the unusual form of our attire. Here was a final nail hammered into my frenzied skull, a freshly jolting shock to underline all the others: the date. Half a century away from the Dyalls' house and from Norton Place.

Friday 9th August 1902

I am confronted with contradictions of such enormity that I can barely keep from screaming. On one side: I am Edward Albert Towns. I have always been so. I remember no other life. I had no occasion to question the nature of that life until it vanished. Nothing whatsoever has changed in my basic physiognomy, my voice, by bearing, my stature, my termperament. I cannot recall a single event in the life of Herbert Farley. Not one. Neither do I recognise the names or faces of anyone within Herbert Farley's sphere.

Yet…

On the other side: I am Herbert Farley. Upon leaving Miss Searle, Mr Harris and Mr Karvitch, I returned to my lodgings. Without needing to ask the address or directions! An address different to that of Edward Towns, but rooms of very similar comforts and affordability. Towns has – had? – an agreeable old landlord called Collins. Farley has an agreeable old landlady called Vereker.

The pages on which I write these words are bound in the selfsame notebook I currently use – that I used? – yet every entry before my last one, despite being written in my own hand, is completely alien to me. Last night, unable to rest, I looked back through previous diaries. The biographical points of comparison, alluded to by Harris, are striking.

How is this possible?

I have eluded Mrs Vereker's kind enquiries about my distracted and confused state by saying I'm suffering from a touch of sciatica. If only I were!

Having found a map among 'my' effects, in precisely the same place I might always have kept one, I set out after breakfast to establish some information about my new surroundings. No sooner was I walking the streets than a further worrying – comforting? – piece of evidence presented itself on the H. Farley side of the equation: unless E. Towns, resident of the year 1850, had – has? – the ability to foretell the future, then I – he – should have been baffled at the occasional sight of an automobile, or the display of gramophones in a shop window. But I was not.

How is this possible?

According to my map, the web of local thoroughfares matches my memories almost exactly. However Scott Street, where E. Towns lived, is an industrial site and bears no sign of having once been residential. Norton Place, it turns out, is only a short walk from my new home. The road, and the central garden, are as I expected them to be, but the houses are of a different style entirely, and of greater age than those I know. Knew.

I proceeded to the district and county records offices. I was born and brought up within five miles of the spot on which I stood, and Agatha likewise, so our presence must be registered here, if anywhere.

With the help of one of the curators, I searched through innumerable ledgers, files and documents. I could find no trace of anyone named Towns, not in any year between 1800 and 1875. Neither could I find Agatha, nor her family, nor any friend whose name came to mind. There had been a Mr Dyall, listed as a trader in antiques, but as he'd died in 1845 he was clearly not either of the gentlemen I'd met. It seems that a London Mesmeric Infirmary had been established nearby, and in the same month and year as my 'departure', but there was no trace of any Clements in connection with it. The facility closed down in 1852. With a brain in turmoil and a heart as heavy as lead, I returned to my rooms.

Reluctantly, I am forced to a conclusion with is both inescapably logical and the cause of intense personal grief: Harris is correct. My past and my identity as Edward Albert Towns are pure fabrication. Why, and how, my own mind has played this horrible trick on me is a mystery. I can only hope that Harris is also right about my proper memories reasserting themselves in due course. I can only hope that their truth and accuracy are worthy of the same trust I have – I *had* – in those of Towns. It is clear that Towns and Farley have much in common and that their experiences bear multiple points of comparison, yet many minor details must forever remain unverified and doubtful since I, whether as Towns or as Farley, have no living relatives who might be consulted on such issues.

I am in a strange and terrible limbo. All available evidence, here and now, says I am Herbert Farley. But my every inner instinct insists I am not.

And I am dreadfully afraid. What if Farley's memories reveal him – me! – to be concealing crimes or engaging in vile pursuits? What if I don't want his – my! my! my! – life, and never will?

My heart aches for Agatha. I would give entire worlds to hold her hand once more.

Saturday 10th August 1902

My memories as Edward Towns from 1850 are utterly unchanged. I am becoming nervous about leaving my rooms, even for an hour, for fear of learning something about Farley's life – *my* life! *damnation and hellfire*! – of which I don't approve. His deeds are my deeds, his sins are my sins.

Mr Karvitch called on me this morning to check on my wellbeing and express his regret that our amateur dabbling in the spirit world had caused me distress. It was kind of him, and I tried hard to give an impression of steady recovery. I did not wish to ask him outright about how we'd come to know each other and so forth, because I have no energy or enthusiasm to engage in a conversation which would reignite his wild speculation. We took tea together and spoke for a while, but I was unable to glean more than a few scraps of fresh information.

Wednesday 14th August 1902

No change! I feel I am living in a nightmare facsimile of myself!

I read various newspapers – *The Times*, *The London Daily Examiner* and others – and I understand coverage of the

Imperial Preference arrangements and the war in South Africa without any conscious previous knowledge of them. Twice I have received letters from people of whom I've never heard but whose correspondence makes perfect sense to me. All this, with my mind *fixed* and *steadfastly* that of a man who does not exist!

From Harris, I have borrowed the volume on spiritualism he had at his side last week. I have found it to be no more than superstitious nonsense, of no help whatsoever. And I am happy to say so, since at least it marks *one* difference of opinion between Towns and Farley!

My dearest Agatha haunts my every thought. The more firmly I try to convince myself that she is not *gone* but *never was*, the more violently my mind rebels at such cowardly betrayal. I simply cannot dismiss what is so deeply embedded in my affections. I cannot give her up.

The shadow of madness darkens my every hour. The world seems strained and tenuous, increasingly unreal.

Unreal? How can I even distinguish between fact and fancy any more? By what method? By what wayward, twisted science? Without the continuities of life and memory, what am I?

Thursday 15th August 1902

I have visited Harris, I have made him see the urgency and sincerity of my position, and he has agreed to mesmerise me again. Tomorrow. Under more carefully operated conditions this time. And for purely therapeutic purposes, entirely separated from spiritualist goals.

I told him plainly: I cannot continue to exist in this fog of uncertainty and contradiction. I cannot. No matter what the chances of a favourable outcome, no matter what risks I may run. When I am in a hypnotic trance, Harris is to command my unconscious mind to restore Farley's memories and to erase those belonging to Towns.

These efforts must succeed, or I will succumb to despair. The loss of everything I knew, Agatha most of all, is agony beyond endurance. If Farley's memories prove to be unrecoverable, if I am left without any past at all, then so be it. I would rather be set adrift, with past and present forever unreconciled, than face this torment.

Tuesday 2nd November 1956

There was no sensation of transition at all. I walked home after requesting that Harris re-mesmerise me, I wrote in my diary, I sat with a book for a while, in a vain attempt to distract myself from the storm in my head, I turned a page—

—and was in a semi-recumbent position, on a padded lounger not unlike a dentist's chair, with a tightly fitting helmet encasing most of my head. From the helmet trailed dozens of electrical cables connected to banks of equipment covered in chunky, heavy duty dials and switches. Needles twitched inside a dozen meters, oscilloscopes flickered, valves glowed.

A clipped man in a white laboratory coat trundled himself across the grey lino floor tiles towards me, propelling himself on a creaking swivel chair. "We thought we'd better pull you out early, Charles, the readings were getting a bit hairy and you were showing signs of excess psychological stress."

A crawling feeling of mental nausea, cold terror mixed with absolute dread, overwhelmed my senses. My whole body began to tremble and my eyesight seemed to tunnel for a moment as I fought a sharply prickling sensation which flushed rapidly across my skin.

"What in God's name—" I croaked.

"Easy does it," said the scientist, adjusting the stubby pipe in his mouth. "You'll be pleased to hear the psychological stress was well worth it, we got almost everything. The gaffer will be delighted! A few more results like this and they won't dare cut our funding. That was a stroke of genius, jumping ahead like that half way through. What prompted you to do it?"

"It was… accidental," I muttered.

I heard a tapping of heels. A beautiful Asian woman came into view, a clipboard in one hand and a glass of water in the other. "Accidental?" she said. "The temporal connection went haywire at that jump point, you were lucky not to encounter feedback. Here, drink this, you've been sweating profusely."

I looked down at myself. I was wearing a very plain pair of grey trousers and a simple white shirt. From my neck hung a thin, dark blue tie. Shakily, I swallowed a gulp or two of water. The helmet was pulled from my head, leaving my hair cold and matted with perspiration.

My heart was galloping like a runaway carriage. I felt as if my brain had turned to solid rock, so numb were my thoughts. Even so, it was perfectly clear that I was transposed forward in time, again! What was not clear was whether this was the result of re-hypnotism, or some fresh delusion, or the final unveiling of reality? With great difficulty, I held my torn nerves as best I could and decided to adopt a systematic approach to my situation.

"What is the date, may I ask?" My voice wavered with fear.

"Don't worry, Dr Stubbs," smiled the woman, "you were under for only ninety minutes, I promise you. It's still Monday."

"I mean the month and year."

They both turned from attending to the machinery all around us and frowned at me. The man pulled a condensed face. "Uh-oh, there may have been some feedback after all. It's the first of November, Charles. Nineteen fifty-six."

"Yes. Of course," I said, forcing a smile. I shuddered.

He nodded and seemed reassured. "It'll take a while to get all this data tabulated, but I'm pretty certain we'll be able to, drum roll please, extract some actual visuals. It's a gold mine. Congratulations, Charles."

As he spoke, he ran a practised eye over a long feed of paper emitted from a buzzing, rasping mechanism in the corner. "The jump you made, that was to August of 1902. At that point the Subject waaaaas…" He walked his chair across to a bank of clicking numerical readouts. "…Was the ripe old age of eighty-three. Was there any noticeable—"

"What Subject was this?" I said.

"Our Mr Edward Towns," he said. He suddenly gave me that doubtful look again. "I'm dreadfully sorry, Charles, I'm letting the excitement of the moment run away with me. You must be exhausted and thoroughly addled. You do look rather washed out. Get a few hours' sleep while the boffins crunch the numbers, yes?"

The mention of the name Edward Towns set my mind spinning with even greater speed and stomach-turning descent. "Yes," I said feebly, heaving myself out of the lounger. "I'll return shortly."

The woman had already gone, it seemed. I stepped out into a very long, narrow corridor, decorated in a similar institutional style to the research room I'd just left: high ceilings, metal pendant lights shaped like flying saucers, creaking floors spread with sagging, colourless carpet. People walked back and forth, wearing either lab coats or severely featureless dark suits. One or two greeted me with a "good afternoon, Dr Stubbs."

And I knew where I was going. Of course I did! I had a room on the building's residential floor, with a small bathroom attached. Approaching it, I rooted in my pocket for the key.

I locked the door behind me. I stood with my back to it, my eyes closed, shaking hands clasped to my face.

Oh, help me. Help me, I beg of you. If there is any god in any heaven who can hear my plea, then in the name of mercy help me!

I ran into the bathroom, to the age-flecked mirror hung over the wash basin. My own face. Mine. Nobody else's. Mine. Then who am I?

Panic shook my limbs and my mind. I threw myself onto the pale blue bed covering and curled up tightly. My whole world became the tiny, enclosed, airless space formed between eyes, knees and arms.

I want to go home. To my life. To my beloved Agatha. I don't belong here!

But am I not Herbert Farley?

But am I not Dr Charles Stubbs?

I must be Dr Charles Stubbs, his world is here, real, solid, existing. I am on his bed in his room. Everyone here knows that I am Dr Charles Stubbs.

But I am not. I am not.

I must have slept out of sheer fatigue. When consciousness slowly returned I found myself laying outstretched, face pressed into the musty candlewick bedspread. I sat up, my whole body aching, and removed the dull fur from my mouth and brain with a wash and a change of clothes. By the alarm clock at my bedside it was 4:30am. A fat central heating radiator hissed and popped beneath the window, from which was visible a landscape of hills, ghostly in moonlight.

Feeling slightly more settled, I looked through the heap of papers stacked on a small desk by the wardrobe. Amongst them, grouped together, were my diaries. Edward Towns's diaries, all of them. The pages were yellowed with age and the ink a good deal faded in many places, but I knew them instantly.

I found the current volume. Or rather, the most recent volume. This volume. Every entry was exactly as I remembered it, including the final one dated 15th August 1902. I stared at it, dumbfounded, for what seemed like days.

How is this possible?

I have now added *this* entry after it. I *will* keep a record. I am *not* mad.

Wednesday 3rd November 1956

I have ceased all capacity for astonishment, so tenuous had my hold on actuality become. I discovered that the papers on my desk included a loosely bound file headed *Subject: Edward Albert Towns 1819-1904*. In it were extensive notes on my activities throughout 1849, based on my diaries, along with various other documents including the letter from Agatha dated 10th January 1850 in which she invited me to the musical evening at the home of her friend Mrs Dyall. Also, the official certificate of my death. There was nothing relating to my life after January 1850 – where did it go? There was no acknowledgement of my diary entries for 1902 – had they even been here?

What, now, am I to believe? In complete contradiction to the proof I had that Edward Towns did not exist, here was proof that he did. That *I* did! Did I? Do I?

With a burst of fury I swept all the papers off the desk. They fluttered and scattered across the room. I sat with my arms flung around my head, rocking to and fro, my heart threatening to tear itself from my chest and my breath labouring in short, moaning gasps.

At 9am, having tidied myself up, I went back to the research room. The scientist from yesterday, I still don't know his name, was there, sipping from a cup of tea while filling in paperwork.

"Ah, Charles, are you yourself again?"

"I am, thank you," I muttered.

"Good, good." He arm gave an angular jerk so he could peer at his wristwatch. "We should be getting one of the visuals we were hoping for any minute now."

"I have… I've been thinking," I said cautiously. "About Edward Towns."

"Feeling a bit of an identity mix-up?" he said. "You said you might. Don't you remember?"

"No," I said.

"You said you might say *that*, too! I'm to remind you of the Stubbs Patent-pending Post-Contact Self-Certainty Principle. To wit, question one, are you having any difficulties understanding the current idiom? Modes of speech? Modern phraseology?

"No."

"Quite. Lampshades shaped like flying saucers et cetera. Question two, do you find anything strange or inexplicable about this room and all its technology?"

"No."

"Ergo, you are a person from, and of, the present day. You were hypnotically psycho-displaced onto a Subject in the past, and then brought back. Not the other way around. Never fear, you are Dr Charles Stubbs."

This is exactly the reasoning by which I had confirmed I was Herbert Farley. It is irrefutable. Almost self-evident.

Yet false. Or I cannot be Edward Towns. It must be false.

My bones turned to water. The scientist checked his watch again, as his female counterpart arrived brandishing a sheet of paper.

"We have it," she beamed. "The quality is a little ropey, but we have it."

The man all but snatched it from her hands. Joy lit his face. He looked from her, to me, to the paper and back again. Eyes glittering, he thrust it into my hands. "Here you are, Charles. Extracted from the raw impulses in your mind, via the quantum field, as piggy-backed through the eyes of a man who died half a century ago."

On the paper was an image composed of ones and zeros, many thousands of them. Parts of the picture were indistinct, as if out of focus, but most of it was rendered in detail. It showed a group of people, seated and standing, looking away to the right. The most prominent figure was a woman in an evening dress, with curly hair and a pensive expression on her face.

It was Agatha. Captured in the precise moment when I glanced at her admiringly, during the harpsichord recital so long ago. So long ago. My dearest. Lost.

I fled. Ignoring the cries of my colleagues I ran to my room, yelling at the top of my voice the whole way. Scrambling through the papers I'd scattered on the floor, I found the current volume of my diary – *this* volume – and held it firmly to my chest.

This is all I have. This is my existence. Whoever I am, whatever I am. There *is* a me.

I took a pen. I climbed out of the window, across a flat section of roof, down to the grass, and ran. I found a concealed spot, a bench by a river. I wrote this down.

Who am I? Where is my life? Am I nowhere? Am I the invention of my own head? Who am I? Who am I? Who am I? Who am I?

Monday 8th September 2007

"And you begin to wake now, James. As you wake, you feel relaxed and refreshed. You are fully awake in three, two, one…"

I opened my eyes to find looming over me a primly immaculate lady, skin wrinkled like a mountain range and pebbled glasses far larger than her face could accommodate. She was sitting at my side, writing in a jotter pad. I was lying on a leather couch, my head resting on a paper antimacassar, one arm clamped around this diary.

I leaped to my feet. A large office, dressed to imitate a domestic setting. Outside, a city of enormous height.

"What circle of Hell is this?" I shouted, both unwilling and unable to keep myself in check any longer.

"James, I can see you feel upset—"

"Upset?" I yelled. "Upset? My name is not James!"

She remained completely at ease. "You're not James Collins? Then Dr Charles Stubbs perhaps? Or Herbert Farley?"

"What?" I spluttered, my temper rising into frenzy. I paced the floor, trembling, filled with the urge to smash things. "No! No! No!"

This was my psychotherapist, apparently! We'd had a session of hypnotherapy. Past life regression, no less!

"Why? What the hell for? Why?"

"To help you overcome your morbid fixation with that diary you carry around. I think you've made excellent progress today. You've uncovered two distinct incarnations in the early and mid-twentieth century."

"Stubbs and Farley? I am neither! Do you hear me? Nor am I James Collins! My name is Towns!"

"Not according to your subconscious, you're not."

I stalked the room like a caged animal, waving my diary at her. "Time travel experiments in the 1950s? Are you insane? Edwardians talking to the dead? It's impossible! Poppycock! Rubbish! I know I doubted myself, but I was wrong, I must be Edward Albert Towns! I must be! Must be!"

Exhaustion seeped into my rage. "I don't know any more!" I wailed. "I can't tell. It's all churned up in my head! I'm trapped outside my life, no way back, no control, no free will."

"You've told me," said my psychotherapist calmly, flipping through her jotter, "that free will is an illusion caused by not being able to foretell the future."

She must have pressed a button. At that moment, two nurses marched in, both of them built like concrete bunkers. "Time for a rest now, Mr Collins," said the first one.

"Come on, Jim, let's show your friends in the Day Room how cooperative you can be," said the second one.

They gripped my upper arms like vices. I kicked and twisted. I screamed.

"My name is Towns! I am real! Get me out of this nightmare! Get me out! Get me out! I want to go home! I want my Agatha!"

Saturday 20th Fivemonth 2090

"You! Preston! Nero Preston! Stop squibbling about like a fucking worm! You've broken the connection again!" They shout at me. This place is cold, derelict, noisy. I keep getting the wiring wrong. "Redial the psychomotor, Preston! What the fuck is the matter with you?"

Twoday 32nd Sevenmonth 2139

I don't know any more. I'm tired. I don't know.

Fourday, 18th Nine 2181

Please help me.

Boneweed bowed before the king and queen. His voice, even when intended to sound sweet, was harsh and scratchy. "Curiosity will not give me back my tongue tonight, it seems," he said. "I must ask if the court's spellhurler is as deadly a trickster as sinister rumour would imply?"

The assembled courtiers tried to gasp in shock, but the ever-deepening enchantment into which they were slipping allowed them only a horrified sigh. To mention the royal djinn once, without written leave, was to risk execution. To mention it twice was without precedent.

Croaknot slowly turned to the king, fearing the worst, but King Harlèd seemed as calm as the waters of Lake Solid. He swayed jerkily on his throne. "You may answer him, Croaknot," he said at last.

"Your Magnificence," bowed Croaknot. He composed himself for a moment, as if about to reveal some dreadful personal secret. "The Djinn Of Continuum," he wheezed, "has enjoyed the protection of the Crown since its capture seven hundred and ninety-seven suncycles past. Of the nine wishes bestowed by treaty upon its present owner, His Exulted Glory King Harlèd, five have been used. One to repel plague, one to repel military invasion thereby establishing the security of the Inner Realms. However, numerical discrepancy revealed that three further wishes – made before the setting up of the Guidance Quorum For Wish Unambiguosityness – must have changed the very nature of the world itself, since there are no records, no memories, no traces of what was altered. The djinn is therefore categorised as a treacherous, deceitful menace to public order. Should it ever escape, the end of all things will follow."

Boneweed cast a careful eye around the ballroom and around the king in particular. His plan would have only one chance of success. His spell needed to grip them all just a little tighter...

Unwanted Callers
Will Be Killed

Hallo? Yes? What? Hang on, let me undo the door chain. There! I'm sorry, what did you say?

You like my Unwanted Callers sign? Ha! Thank you, well, we get so many sales people knocking on doors around here, and shifty buggers saying they'll clean your guttering or pretending this and that to size up your security, well, I thought it best to try to put off as many of them as possible.

Hmm? You've not come here to sell me anything? Well, that a relief! Ha ha ha. Hospital insurance? Oh, no, my health is fine. Look, it's very cold out today, why don't you come inside? That's better, cut out the wind and the noisy road, eh? Go on through.

Do excuse the mess. Just step over those. I'd make a joke about it being my cleaning lady's day off, but I don't have one. A cleaning lady, I mean.

An artist? I am indeed! Was it the ink all over my clothes or the ink all over the floor that gave it away? Ha ha ha. Yes, move those books and you can sit there. Hmm? Oh, that's OK, just scrape it off on the chair.

Oh yes, every one of these drawings hung here is mine. Well, years, years. I've devoted my life to art, all my energies. Would you like some tea? Thought I had a biscuit in this pocket, but I must have eaten it, never mind. I'm afraid you've caught me between shower-and-laundry days. No tea? You're sure? I think I have some meat from last week in the fridge if you'd like a sandwich? No?

Pardon? You find my drawings interesting? Very kind of you to say so. Evocative, yes, that's a good word for them. Vile, my ex-wife called them. Vile and repellent. Can't please 'em all, eh? Ha. I'm so glad you appreciate them, they mean a great deal to me. Ooo, um, must be over a hundred on these walls alone. Consistent in theme, yes, quite right, you've obviously got a good eye for such things.

This one here, for example. Let me just unpin it from the wall. Closer look. There we are. This one here is... Hmm? Healthcare needs? Don't have any. I'm a little spindly and unkempt, but fit as a fiddle, thank you. This one here is a personal favourite. By the way, all these around us are pen and ink on hot-pressed one-twenty-gram, which I cut to size myself. I use mainly black ink with one or two colours used sparingly for highlighting and emphasis. The little red streaks on this one, you see here, yes? As it's emerging from Hell. Yes, it does look very beetle-like. I like all the serrations on the limbs. And the human figures, there, hiding in the bushes, they're designed so that you only notice their presence after you've been looking at the picture for a few seconds, so you suddenly get a changed sense of scale and realise the creature is about twice their height. I think it's the sense of menace, the feeling of tearing claws, that makes this a favourite. Hmm? Oh, many hours, I couldn't tell you exactly how long. Over several days, of course. I have to sleep occasionally, ha ha ha.

Now, that one, above the radiator, that's a very interesting one. If you look to the right of the one with the centipede eating a... yes, the one with a face in its belly. That's an interesting one because it's based on a demon from medieval European folklore. This demon was said to steal people from their beds in the middle of the night if they'd forgotten to wear their undies or something like that, I can't recall. No that's a second mouth, see the teeth? It goes right across the chest like that so the demon's got extra gut room for stuffing in peasants. Absolutely, the stuff of nightmares, yes.

I'm quite keen on... Nooo, don't you worry, it's quite alright, plenty of time, lots to see yet. I'm sure you'll appreciate this large picture here, behind you. One I'm really rather proud of, in actual fact. I drew it a long time ago, must be twenty years at least, I should say, more probably thirty but, even now, every time I look at it, I can't help but feel a certain glow.

Hmm? The eyes follow you? Yes, they do, don't they. Well, they would. This is also based on specific legends, it depicts one of the ancient serpent goddesses, the green picks out the light reflecting off her scales. I always think there's something really beguiling about her shape, the way her arms and fingers coil, that hint of a smile behind her forked tongue. I can gaze at her for entire afternoons. What? Oh, well, ha ha, that's her intended effect!

No, every one is different, each drawing is unique. I'm sorry, why do I what? Oh, well, I suppose in common with many an artist I like to imagine the subject chooses me rather than me choosing it. If you see what I mean. It's my calling, you might say, it's my vocation, my passion, perhaps even my compulsion. I know what, come with me, I'll show you my studio.

No trouble at all, I assure you. It's a genuine pleasure to meet a fellow art lover. Come along, my studio is right behind these curtains. Et viola! Do excuse the mess. Once again. No, I'm simply one of life's untidy slobs, I'm afraid. No excuse. I devote all my time to my compositions, you see. I work in here because the light is so much better, even with the garden as overgrown as it is, it's south facing. In any case, I'd never get this huge drafting table into the front room, ha ha ha!

Before I begin a drawing, I sit here quietly, with my eyes closed, and I attune myself to the unseen forces in the ether. I've got quite good at it, over the years. I think myself into the darkness, and then it's as if the darkness itself extends a little tendril into my brain and swirls it around. It shows me what waits, out of sight. It places forbidden sights into my eyes. And then, to my delight, the picture emerges from the paper, simply through the movement of my pen. Every tiny detail, bit by bit, seems to flow through me from mind to hand. Hmm? No, I never do sketches or rough versions, each piece expresses itself finished and complete. Whole. They say, don't they, the essence of a great creative mind is knowing when something is just exactly right, whether it's brush strokes on canvas, words on paper, notes on a stave. An instinct for what is true and meaningful.

What? Yes, yes, I agree, but then great art, in whatever form, visual or otherwise, takes on true existence, entirely separate from its creator. Don't you think? When it speaks to us, when it warms the emotions, and does so needing no context or explanation, then it has become an entity in its own right. With a life all its own. It's why art is the human race's only worthwhile achievement. Because it reaches beyond us.

Do I sell many? Good grief, no. Hmm? No, in fact, quite the reverse, because I could never bear to part with a single one. They look after me, emotionally, just as I look after them. My drawings are of far more personal value than any amount of money that could possibly be offered. Ah, perhaps you'll understand when you see some of my most recent projects, I've got them here somewhere, um, would you lift up that bowl and plate? Yesterday's breakfast. These pictures are studies of segmented tapeworms with different... Pardon?

Oh. A forgotten appointment? Not at all, not at all. I find many a caller, after a while, suddenly becomes both busy and absent-minded, our chats must be thoroughly absorbing. That's it, back past the curtains and through the front room.

Yes, the door out to the hallway is indeed locked. Well, it's been such fun meeting you and thank you again for taking the trouble to... Locked, that's right. Well, so you can't get out, ha ha!

Ah, your expression tells me you've seen the change in the pictures, well spotted! Forgive me, I do enjoy the look on a caller's face when they notice, it gives me a wonderful feeling of validation. As an artist. It's very flattering when others acknowledge your work being beyond mere ink and paper.

No, no, the pictures haven't become blank, each creature and demon is still here in this room with us. When they move towards you, you'll... that's it. Oh dear, they did give you a fright, didn't they! Don't worry, they'll eat up every scrap of you. If you could, though, do try not to bleed on the books. Hmm? Well, to be fair, the sign on the door did warn you.

Boneweed danced a little dance. Now his word-enchantment was past the point of reversal, and the dreaming fog around the minds of his listeners was beginning to lift. Where there had been an easily-dismissed aching in their limbs, now there was pain, sharp and creeping. But they could neither move nor cry out. Where there had been peculiar stirrings inside them, now there were distinct objects being rearranged, bones and muscles being replaced. The crucial moment of Boneweed's plan had arrived.

"Now then," he said, toes tapping with excitement. "I'd like to meet the djinn."

As it turned, the king's head click-click-clicked. "Then you shall. Croaknot, go to the lower vaults. Unlock them. Bring the djinn here to us."

Croaknot hesitated, terror and doubt battling across his wrinkled features. "Immediately, Your Eminent Transcendence." He scurried away with impeccable delicacy. Being used to the hard discomforts of great age, he paid little attention to all the extra pains he was experiencing.

Welcome To Club Xingfú

My heartbeat was fluttering like a hummingbird and my breath came in grating gasps that hurt my chest. I hadn't slowed down for a couple of miles or more and the exertion of running at full tilt was catching up with me.

I turned a corner into a broad alleyway, a canyon between two back-to-back terraces of smart city centre shops. Huge tip-up bins lined each side. I ducked down beside one to hide while I got my breath back.

It was close to 1 a.m. Yellowed security lights, high above, threw meagre pools into the deep dark. Sounds of life and traffic were a distant blur. I sat on gritty, rubbish-strewn concrete and watched my breath clouding in jets with every heave of my lungs.

They weren't chasing me, I was sure of that. Ninety per cent sure. Eighty. It was fright alone that had set me running. That unexpected yell of "Hoi!" behind me as I exited through the back of the building, it had cut into my nerves like ice, pushed me hard into the night. Now it echoed inside my head, endlessly, relentlessly.

They can't have seen my face. They couldn't even know that I knew where they were. If they'd recognised me, that "Hoi!" would have been "Oi! Mozza!" instead. Surely? By *pure chance* they must have spotted my shape creeping out! Shit shit shit shit. I'd planned it *so well*! Shit! Shit! Shit! They wouldn't be accusing one another of taking the money, as planned, because now they knew someone else had sneaked in and taken it. It'd be suspected people's heads they'd be kicking in, not each other's. They'd work their way down to me eventually. A week or two. I'd need to cover my tracks and fix an alibi. A very, very good one.

I clutched at the bulges inside my coat, three bricks of banknotes, and I grinned. More cash than I'd ever had at one time in my life, ever.

I staggered to my feet and peeped over the top of the bins. Nobody was about. My legs felt like water and I had to hug myself to stop the shakes, but I was wide awake and fizzing with equal quantities of excitement and worry.

I pointedly strolled, as steadily as I could, out of the alley and along the brightly lit shop fronts. A street or two later all the pubs and bars were closed up for the night, but as I passed a row of nondescript buildings I glanced across the road and saw a long, thin illuminated sign, only just visible above street level, behind a set of old-fashioned iron railings.

"Club Xingfú."

I suddenly remembered hearing about this place, although I couldn't recall when or how. Or I read about it somewhere? Or I was told about it by someone? A definite memory that this was a private club where – the words seemed to form themselves in my head – where may be found refuge from a troubled world, new members welcome.

I crossed to the railings and stood looking over them, down into a narrow stone stairwell, like the entrance to a basement flat. The sign shone softly above an open doorway, its heavy, sculpted door held ajar. Beyond, even in the gloom, I could see pristine carpeting in a rich shade of purple.

Scuffing down the steps, I expected to meet a bouncer or a doorman, but none appeared. I leaned over the threshold, inquisitive head forward, and after a moment or two the rest of me followed. Inside, discreet wall lights shaped like flames emerged from plaster dragons' heads. My footsteps made no sound at all on the carpet as I descended a long, coiling staircase. Here and there I ran a finger along the oddly up-and-down handrail that curved beneath the lights.

I could smell alcohol and perfume. Music drifted, an eerie Far Eastern melody of high, plucked notes and weeping strings. I emerged into a wide, low-ceilinged room with a central circular drinks bar. There were innumerable booths and white-clothed tables divided up by dark lattice screens carved out in Chinese patterns, deep shadows falling between patches of light that seemed to come from nowhere in particular, identically uniformed waiters, walls richly textured and black.

The place was quite full, and a hum of voices hazed the air. It hiccuped for a moment when I walked in, all eyes flicking at me and away again.

I went over to the bar. The immaculate barman placed a paper coaster and a glass of vodka in front of me before I could speak. I reached into my coat but he shook his head. "You pay when you leave." I took a sip and turned to face the room.

I don't know how I got talking to the scruffy sod. He was sitting alone, at a sectioned-off table by the wall opposite the stairs, and then I was sitting there too.

He nodded an eager smile at me. "Thought I recognised a kindred spirit," he said. His voice crackled like an old vinyl record. "You're here through bad luck." A statement, not a question..

That "Hoi!" was still raw and circling around my brain. I nodded back. "Yes, I s'pose I am." We introduced ourselves and took a companionable swig of our drinks. A passing waiter silently topped up his glass, and mine.

I'd never met anyone as pitiable as that scruffy sod. His face was lined with a lifetime's events, sagged and jowly, with thinned hair so flat and shaped I thought it might be a wig. His skin seemed puffy and textured, like an overripe orange, but also colourless in a way which should normally have been hidden by the dimmed lighting. His mottled fingers, adorned with several rings, were knitted around his drink. His clothes were loosely tossed over his meagre frame. Age aside, his manners were of an earlier generation, when working men wore their only suit to the pub on Sundays and everyone owned a hat.

He was so obviously broken. His eyes betrayed an inner bitterness which wanted to blaze but had barely enough energy to flicker. A man defeated, tired, resentful.

"Tell you what, mate," he said, as if producing a surprise present for a little boy he knew wouldn't like it, "I've got a business proposition for you."

"Sorry," I said, "now's really not the time—"

"More sort of a bargain," he said quickly, his fingers itching to either plead or grab. "A trade. Yes, a trade."

He seemed so wretched I felt I had to hear him out. "Trading what?"

His smile exposed peculiarly small teeth. "Bad luck brought you here, so I'm guessing you're on your uppers? Maybe, potentially, in a lot of trouble if things don't go your way?"

I paused. "True."

He gulped his drink and nodded sharply. "Same for me, one time back in the day, exactly the same. I was about your age, too, about thirty years ago—"

Only thirty?

"—and I got myself into a really bad situation. Back then, I worked for the Mills family, you know who I mean?"

The city's nastiest gangsters.

"This was back before Billy took over and sharpened up the whole operation. I was a big bloke in those days, believe it or not, handy with my fists, and there was this beady-eyed runt, an accountant everyone called Ratty, who the bosses thought was screwing them over. I was told, on the quiet, to take him somewhere and smack the truth out of him. Not kill him, because he had friends in the banks or something. I was to scare him shitless, get the truth out of him, but they said if I topped him I'd end up in the same hole in the ground.

"I drove him out to the woods, in the middle of the night. He kept trying to bite through the cords around his wrists. I dragged him out of the car and up a hill, into the trees, and he's kicking and shouting and offering me money.

"I start whacking his arms and legs with a crowbar, but he wouldn't talk. I can still hear those screams. His damn shrieking wound me up and I hit him hard on the back of the head.

"He just dropped to the ground, like a stone. Gone.

"Then it was my turn to shit myself. The Mills would put a bullet in me as soon as they found out. I sat there, sweating, in a panic. I couldn't run, I had no cash. And people knew me. I couldn't even tell the Mills whether he'd really been robbing them or not. I couldn't even bury the bastard, I hadn't brought a bloody shovel with me, had I?

"I covered him up with leaves. I wandered around the woods, planning things that just got madder and madder. I was blubbing like a baby so through all the tears I wasn't sure what I was looking at, at first. I wiped my eyes with my sleeves and even then I thought I was either dreaming or I'd cracked up.

"There was a fireplace. Like you get in old houses, with a mantelpiece and everything. Right there, between the trees. There were logs burning and two big red leather armchairs, the sort with high backs and that dimpled look to them, you know what I mean?

"Someone was sitting in one of them. I went closer, not quite believing it was all real. By then, I was so scared of what would happen later I'd have petted a crocodile without blinking. This someone held out a hand towards the other chair. It spoke, and its voice was soft and smooth, it said, please sit with me."

"It?" I said, frowning.

The scruffy sod nodded. "I mean, it looked like a human being, but it wasn't one. It was dressed like a human, very smart, and when it talked it was like hearing notes played on, what-they-called, woodwind instruments."

"How do you know it wasn't human, if it spoke to you?"

"It told me it wasn't. But it didn't need to. There was something *wrong* about it. Off. Abnormal. It made my flesh crawl, even though it was very calm and friendly. Then I was sitting in the other armchair and the heat from the fireplace made my cold hands and face feel prickly.

"It said to me, bad luck has brought you here. I didn't know what to say, I just said yes. And you face a hazardous future, it said. I said yes. It said, I can offer you a way out, a life charmed against all misfortune. And it told me who it was. It was so long ago, and I was so scared, I can't remember a lot of it—"

When I was very young, my parents were brought to such misery by my presence that they thought I must be a changeling, a twisted creation left by faeries in place of their own human child. They were right. I am. What became of their real child, I do not know.

They didn't like me. I didn't like them. I suspect they were unwilling, for some time, to believe they harboured an evil imp, but my sullen disposition and the trembling wariness of my peers must have forced the truth upon them in the end. I expect it was my father who saw it first, he was always the credulous, emotional one.

For many years, growing up, I didn't understand who and what I am. I didn't want to be different from everyone around me – children don't, do they? – but by the time I reached adulthood I'd learned to value my difference. To celebrate it. To be true to myself.

I came to embrace the truth, that I am a living curse. I am a lodestone of misfortune, an ill omen. My baleful influence extends wherever my attention is turned. I walk in sorrow and decay, where the aeriform threads of chance are mine to command, to gather or scatter as I see fit. I am a god of failure. This is the role for which I was made. As such, I have sought out a place in the world, a niche for myself within humanity.

Thus, I offer you a way out by means of a trade. You will leave here and be free of fate's whims. Chance will favour you, inconspicuously but consistently, for as long as you wish. Your luck will literally change for the better, you will live a life transformed.

In return, you will be required to perform a task. One task only, and once it has been carried out your charmed life will simply continue as before. This task may be demanded of you at any time – tomorrow, next week, next year, or perhaps not until the final hours of your long and happy existence – but demanded of you it will be, sometime.

If you refuse to do as asked, or if you fail to carry it out, then our agreement ends with your immediate death, and the deaths of all your loved ones, and the eternal damnation of your soul, and theirs. There is no knowing what will be required of you, or when the request may come, but it will be a task in the service of Darkness itself, and in Darkness hide the vilest depravities of Hell and the human heart.

"—vile depravity, it said, but I was in such trouble and in such a panic over what might happen that I agreed. I said, what do I do, do I sign on the dotted line in blood? And it gave me this look which made me go cold, this animal look like a spider scuttling to crunch a fly. It said, there is no need, the bargain was struck when you came to my attention and sat beside me."

"And this is the same bargain you're offering me now?" I said, making the effort to humour him.

"But, it works," said the scruffy sod. He seemed to twitch rather than nod, and his lips trembled while his bony hands rotated his glass on the table. "The changeling, whatever it was, was true to its word. I went back into town a nervous wreck, thinking I'd been imagining things or I'd lost the plot. I didn't sleep a wink. Then the next day, the Mills told me they'd found out the accountant was working for a rival gang and now they wanted him dead! I told them I'd sort it, went back, got the body, dumped it outside these rivals' pub as ordered. The law came sniffing around, but I was smelling of roses! I never got charged. I left the Mills and the bad days behind me, I had money, bought a nice house. I never had a day's illness! I even had regular wins of a few hundred quid on the horses and the lottery. I even attracted women! Unbelievable! Me!

"But all the time… I was waiting and wondering. When would that human-shaped thing come back? Or would something else come, some horror crawling out from under the bed? Or would I just get a message out of nowhere? I waited and wondered and fretted about it. Knowing there'd be no warning, pretty soon I was jumping at shadows every minute of the day and night. Every knock on the door would carve up my nerves, every envelope on the mat, every stranger who looked at me for a second too long.

"I wouldn't have felt so jumpy, so bloody terrified, if I'd known what to expect. Darkness, it said. In the service of darkness. I'd been too stupid to think it through properly, for a while. This suffocating fright slowly grew inside me, eating me up, a bit more each day, day after day.

"Vile, it said. Depraved. Vilest depravities of the human heart. What does that mean, these days, when the whole world's turned to shit? Cutting, burning, torturing? Women? Kids? Worse? My brain kept spinning faster and faster, thinking of sickening things, horrible things, horrible, horrible things.

"These years of waiting have finished me. I've had all the luck in the world, like it said I would, a comfortable life, a loving home, but getting gradually louder and louder in my head... bloody torment that never ends. Endless, endless worry and fear, gnawing away, the waiting and waiting and wondering what in Hell's name might turn up."

"And this is how I'll feel if I take up your offer, is it?" I said.

He flinched, suddenly conscious of what he was saying and reigning himself in. He worked spider-like at his glass and he quickly dragged a cuff under his nose. "No, no, mate, no, it's only because I've left it so long, right? I mean, the longer I've left it, the greater the chance of this task turning up, right? I've dithered and tried to put it out of my mind, over and over, but it never goes away and now I've left it so long the tension's unbearable."

He half-laughed and threw the rest of his drink down his throat. An arm with a bottle slid out of the shadows to refill both our glasses. I looked across the table at the scruffy sod, this human wreckage, and despite myself I felt sympathy for him.

"I don't understand how you can offer me the same trade?" I said. "What do you get out of it?"

"Of course, yes, right," he said with care, covering his terror with a mask of strained salesmanship. "There's what you might call a get-out clause. The thing in the woods told me that the bargain can be passed on to someone else. At any time. If you can find someone willing, then they can take it on instead. But you've got to tell them the truth, they've got to be willing, they've got to agree of their own free will. If you pass it on, you lose all the charmed life stuff, you get no more from then on and you're on your own, but the obligation to carry out the task is passed on too. That's what I'm offering you, see. Whatever trouble you've got now, it'll go away—"

"And I'll go mad worrying about a vile and depraved task I might have to do at any minute?"

I could see panic scrambling to be let out from behind his swimming eyes and shaking chin. "No, you see, I left it too long, like I said. I let it get to me, I was greedy for all the good things that were coming my way. I wasn't thinking clearly. But now I've told you about it, you don't need to repeat my mistake. You can get yourself out of any problem but then you'll know to hand it all on to someone else before it gets to you. You need only take the risk for a short time. Or maybe you can live with the risk much better than me? Much better than a snivelling coward like me, I bet you could. It's up to you. You're still young, you've got donkey's years ahead of you, so a fresh start right now might be the best thing. It's just me, I can't do it any more, I let it drag on and get to me. I don't mind losing the protection of the magic spell pixie dust whatever the good bit is, I just want to stop being frightened to death all the bloody time. You know not to make my mistake, you'll find someone to pass it on to when you decide, no bother, I'm sure, right?"

I felt sympathy for the poor relic, but mostly because he was so sad, probably lonely, and clearly out of his tiny mind. One look at his sweating, pleading face was enough to convince me he completely and sincerely believed every word of what he'd told me. Whatever inner world of his own he was stuck in, he wanted out. I could sympathise with that.

"What do I have to do?" I said.

His gaze suddenly fixed on me. "You'll agree? You accept?" he beamed.

"What have I got to lose?" I smiled. "I agree. Cursed or blessed, we're all one or the other, aren't we?"

"Of your own free will?"

"Of my own free will."

He reached across the table and his hands patted repeatedly at mine. "Thank you. Thank you."

"Do we shake on it?"

"No need, you've said yes, that's binding. I can't thank you enough. You've saved my life, truly you have."

"Well, now your mighty shield of fortune has gone, mind you don't go walking under any buses."

He patted my hands, laughing through tears of relief. "I'll be careful. Thank you."

It was getting very late, and now I'd brought a little happiness into a miserable world I needed to find somewhere

I could sleep the rest of the night. We said our goodbyes, I downed the rest of my drink and walked over to the bar.

"Your friend's already paid," said the barman.

I turned to give the scruffy sod a nod and made my way out of the restless fog of voices and aftershaves that still filled the club. The entrance at the top of the curling stairs was as unattended as before. My footsteps, up to street level and across the road, sounded sharp and intrusive in the uncanny quiet of the early hours.

I sometimes wonder, to this day, why I glanced back. I wonder if events might have turned out differently if I hadn't. As I turned, I thought the angles of the sparse street lights and the depthless shadows were playing tricks on me, but I took a couple of slow steps with my blood rapidly chilling and saw I hadn't been mistaken.

There were no steps down to basement level, no illuminated sign, no door. Behind the railings, a horizontal metal grille covered what had been the stairwell. It was the following day when word reached me that confirmed I'd got away with the robbery scot free, and that the money was all mine.

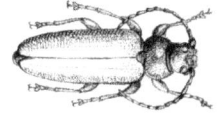

The book closed between Boneweed's flattened hands. At the same moment, Croaknot reappeared, followed by two ragged servitors pushing a tall, heavily reinforced iron cage. The bars of the cage were stout and it rumbled along on iron wheels big enough to remove any chance of tipping over. Symbols in a time-lost language were etched into every surface. Inside the cage was a sealed lining of green glass, so thick it might be mistaken for ice. Inside the glass, a dark shape spun, rolled, glittered.

Croaknot and both the servitors were almost dead. All the way up from the lower vaults, beneath the Spiral Tower, beneath the cellars, beneath the deep foundations, the djinn had used their physical proximity to drain the bonds between their atoms.

The weary servitors bent at the knees but before they could sit down they folded into whispers of grey ash. Croaknot, releasing a delicate cry of anguish, crumbled to the floor with an arm outstretched towards the royal thrones, and became dust.

Boneweed could barely contain his happiness. He took a cautious step closer to the cage. "O Destroyer Of Worlds, I am a penniless and lowly wordist and my sorceries are less than an ocean's drip to your own, but I hope the hex I am calling forth here will please you, if you will but observe it..."

Perkins Saves The Day

There I was, adopting a suave pose at the French windows and feeling hugely confident re: tonight's finals in the 1929 Gadfly Club Darts Tournament, when I noticed something rummy.

"I say," I said, peering out at the well-manicured grounds of Wopley Hall, "it appears Auntie Maude has risen from the grave."

"Risen from the grave?" said Emerald, looking up from her cucumber sandwich like a gazelle caught mid-nibble on the plains of the Serengeti. "How so?"

"You know the family tomb thingummy, down near the boating shed?"

"The one crowded with angels and cherubim and whatnot?"

"The very one. We bunged her in it last Tuesday (complete with carved encomium declaring I Told You It Was My Last Christmas) but there she is biffing across the lawns at full steam! Take a look."

Emerald skipped across the Drawing Room to my side. A dashed attractive girl, is Emerald Fry, all bobbed blonde hair and striking profile. She wrinkled her delightfully petite nose as she stared at the wild figure of Auntie Maude, still a few hundred yards off but making a bee-line for the house. "Oh dear. Even from here she looks awfully cross. But then who wouldn't, if laid to eternal slumber in error?"

"No error, she always has that feral look," I explained. "She is what you'd call a Tough aunt, the sort who wrestles gorillas and chews broken glass by the full moon. We made sure she was fully deceased, explicitly to avoid mistakes, because her afternoon naps have caused more than one footman to run screaming in horror, thanks to her pallor and the way her tongue lolls out between her teeth."

"Oh, so she's definitely undead, then," said Emerald, tapping nervously at her pearl choker.

"Must be, I'm afraid," I tutted, "if only to judge by her shroud, ripped and bloodied like that. If she was still alive, she wouldn't be seen dead in such a state. I wonder what could have caused her reanimation?"

"More to the point, we'd better stop her," said Emerald, "before she goes marauding through the Summer Fête!"

"Oh corks, you're right!" I cried. At that very moment, on the land at the front of the Hall, sun-bronzed villagers would be preparing assorted egg-and-spoon races and refreshment tents for the imminent annual Wopley-On-Avon binge. After the frightful hash I'd accidentally made of last year's festivities, anything in the region of a dust-up at today's gala would find Lord Wopley restringing his tennis racquet with the gizzards of a beloved nephew i.e. me!

But what to do? While beauty and brains come as a matching set with Emerald, my own mental processes are widely acknowledged as outclassed by a goldfish. I leaped for the bell to summon Perkins, my valet, because his mental processes are widely acknowledged to show up Mr Einstein as a bit of a chump.

He appeared instantly – Perkins, that is, not Mr Einstein – and took stock of the situation with lightning efficiency. We three stepped out through the French doors onto the verandah, where we could get a clearer look at the advancing Aunt via Perkins's pocket spy glass.

"Hmm," I declared, when it was my turn, "she's got eyes like golf balls and enough froth at the mouth to be the envy of rabid dogs everywhere."

"Most distressing, Sir," said Perkins.

"But what sort of risen corpse is she?" said Emerald. "Is she the straightforward murdering kind, or is she the kind whose bite issues the bite-ee with an invite to join the living dead?"

"Does it matter?" I said.

"It certainly does!" said Emerald. "If she's Type A, it's simply a question of bopping her on the head before she chews through too many innocent bystanders. If Type B, we'll have to seal off the house and grounds before the whole village, and thence the world, turns into hideous ravening beasts."

"Miss Emerald is quite correct, Sir," said Perkins. "The distinction is one of considerable significance."

"You know, I sometimes think Fate is simply determined to take the razz," I grumbled.

"If I might make a suggestion, Sir? It may be possible to nip this particular difficulty in the bud, as it were, with the aid of His Lordship's shotgun?"

"A topping idea, Perkins!" I said.

"I will endeavour to fetch the firearm with all possible speed, Sir, since I notice Her Ladyship appears to have caught our scent and is heading this way with some eagerness."

Off he went.

"At least we've spotted her before she can do any damage," I mused.

Emerald's lips wiggled. "Might not a ripped and bloodied shroud imply a kill or two?"

Back he came.

Emerald, being a crack shot – what a girl! – swung the shotgun up to her shoulder and took aim while I, being a wilting flower, stuck my fingers in my ears and mulled over that last remark of Emerald's with ever-increasing alarm.

Auntie Maude was barely ten yards away now, snarling and slavering, propelling herself forward with clawed hands outstretched. There was an almighty bang and her head exploded. The air was filled with the aromas of cordite and gristle.

"If you'll allow me, Sir?" murmured Perkins, leaning forward and brushing fragments of skull from my blazer with a handkerchief. "Excellent shot, Miss."

"Thank you, Perkins," said Emerald.

It was at this precise moment when 1) I wished with all my heart and soul that Emerald's remark about the shroud would turn out to be wrong in every possible respect, and 2) Emerald's remark about the shroud turned out to be right.

It may have been the noise of the gun that alerted Auntie's victims to our presence. Suddenly, from the direction of the kitchen garden, stalked Merriman the head groundskeeper and a small flock of under-gardeners, each gnashing his choppers and bleeding from an orifice or two.

"Ah," sighed Emerald. "Type B, I believe."

"Auntie Maude must have buzzed through the greenhouse like a plague of locusts," I gasped.

Emerald snapped open the shotgun. "We're going to need more ammo, Perkins."

The ever-resourceful valet handed her a box of cartridges. "I anticipated just such a contingency, Miss."

She gave him one of her most dazzling smiles. "You really are the complete bee's knees, Perkins."

"Thank you very much, Miss. It may be prudent, Sir, for me to inform the organisers of the fête of events here, in case the sound of gunfire causes undue consternation."

"Indeed, Perkins," I said. "We don't want the village proletariat thinking the red flag's gone up and grabbing their pitchforks."

Perkins gave a deferential dip of the head and departed at a dignified pace, just as Emerald heave-ho'ed the shotgun and blew out the brains of the nearest oncoming corpse. A large splash of grey matter hit my striped trouserings.

These gardeners, much younger and lighter on their feet than Auntie Maude (whose below-stairs soubriquet The Whale Of Wopley was in no way ironical) were therefore moving with a speed which raised the hairs on the back of my neck and froze my spine with the looming fear of having my innards pulled out.

"When you're ready, Emerald," I trembled.

"I'm all fingers and thumbs. Ah! There we are, reloaded."

Bang! Spot on target, and another gardener fell headless. Bang! Slightly off-centre, taking only a mangled half off the fellow's face, but fortunately enough to floor the blighter.

We made a stumbling retreat across the verandah, with the last two snapping at our heels like shipwrecked mariners who've just spotted the last coconut on the island. By way of defence, I picked up a garden chair and heaved it at them. They batted it aside with ease and left it smashed on the paving. Soil-stained fingers grasped at our extremities and hungry mouths lunged.

Bang! Bang! Instantly, my ears felt as if they'd been wedged into Big Ben at noon. I looked down to find bursts of under-gardener scattered at my feet. It took me a moment or two to realise that I was now drenched from tip to toe in blood and entrails.

"You poor lamb," said Emerald, whose House Of Worth dress had fortunately remained untouched by a single corpuscle.

"Poor Perkins, come laundry day," I said, peeling a squashed eyeball off my lapel. "Oh well, at least the whole of civilisation, plus the Wopley-On-Avon fête and my evening at the darts final, are all safe and sound once more."

I was wrong again. Suddenly, a fearful noise erupted from somewhere on the other side of Wopley Hall, a chaos of raised voices from which the only words discernable were 'help' and 'wraaagggh.' Emerald and I exchanged goggle-eyed looks and dashed around the side of the house to see what was going on.

Across the broad lawns, which ran down to the front gates of the estate, were arranged stalls, tombolas and amusements of all kinds, linked arm-in-arm with gently fluttering bunting and the warm aroma of sponge cake. It was a dreamy, bucolic scene, completely ruined by screaming villagers fleeing from the swarm of living dead seething past the gates and up the driveway.

Some of these reanimated visitors were evidently new recruits to the ranks of the undead, as per Merriman and his gardeners, but most of them were literally rotting off the bone. Dressed in filthy rags, they scurried along on creaking, emaciated legs, with their visible skin and muscle either shrunken with time or worm-eaten into a purulent goo. One or two had come apart at the seams and, with skeletal claws, were dragging what was left of themselves across the grass. The rancid smell of the entire mob quickly overwhelmed the delicate fragrances of the tea tent and the vicar's wife's home made jam stall.

"Simply frightful," said Emerald, delicately pinching her nose between two fingers.

Suddenly dashing into view came Smutty Norwood, an old pal of mine and fellow weekend guest at the Hall. He's a sprightly chap, is Smutty, always odds-on favourite when it comes to athletics races and feats of derring-do, so he was off down to the mob before I could even draw breath to shout a warning.

"Look here," I heard him declare, "the fête doesn't officially open until—" The rest was lost in the frenzy as a dozen undead leaped on top of him and sent various organs and yards of intestines flying about the place. Emerald and I winced at the crack of a skull being opened and the noisy noshing of brains.

Perkins glided out of nowhere to appear at my side, bearing a tray of light cocktails. "I took the liberty of preparing restoratives, Sir, since today is proving to be somewhat trying."

"I'll say," I said, handing a drink to Emerald and taking a much-needed gulp of one myself.

"You really are the cat's pyjamas, Perkins," said Emerald.

"Thank you, Miss."

Emerald drooped the shotgun, clearly nonplussed at the sudden expansion of the walking corpse problem. "Looks like this is now as much use as an ice cube in a burning haystack."

"I fear so, Miss. May I advise a rapid retreat to the house?"

As we scampered for safety, I waved my cherry-on-a-cocktail-stick at the swiftly unfolding massacre. "A rampant

Aunt is bad enough, but where on Earth did this lot spring from?"

"I think, Sir, it is more a question of where *under* the Earth they sprang from. If I'm not mistaken, Sir, they are the contents of the village churchyard."

"Egad, Perkins!" I cried. "There must be two or three hundred ancestors laid to rest at St Keyne's! What's caused this craze for resurrection?" Before Perkins could reply, we zipped inside, slammed the front door behind us and started piling nearby furniture up against it.

A booming voice from the foot of the grand staircase made me jump. "You! You've done it again, blast you!"

Lord Wopley stood there with hands on hips and a face like a recently ignited stick of dynamite. A formidable, much-moustachio-ed buzzard, the type who looks as if Nature couldn't decide whether to make a man or a poisonous reptile.

"It's not my fault, Uncle!" I protested.

"You ruined last year's fête, and now you've ruined it again!"

"I haven't!"

"You'll have to apologise to the vicar in no uncertain terms, I can assure you!" He thundered quite a lot more, but it was drowned out by the battering of rotting hands against the front door and the smashing of glass as massed hordes broke in through the French windows.

Emerald, Perkins and I ran upstairs, while Lord Wopley armed himself with his old regimental sword and went off to gather up one or two of the more valuable items from his porcelain figurine collection, intending to lock them out of harm's way in the safe.

It was when we reached the upper landing that I suddenly spied 10-year-old Cousin Egbert, he of the short trousers, grazed knees and runny nose. The ghastly young scourge was peeking over the handrail atop the bannisters, looking sheepish and clutching a large book to his chest.

"What ho, o junior gumboil," I said. "Has that school of yours booted you out again?"

"No such luck," grumbled Egbert. "It's the Summer hols."

At that moment, Perkins indicated an intention to reveal disturbing truths by leaning towards me and quietly issuing a soft, polite cough. "To answer your earlier question, Sir, I have just learned of speculation in the servants' quarters concerning Master Egbert. It seems he's been up to mischief, Sir, having initiated a case of demonic possession among the chambermaids and caused Cook's supply of butter to become sentient."

My eyes narrowed as I beckoned Egbert to my side. "What have you been up to?"

"Experiments," he said. His brevity suggested a guilty conscience.

"Have you raised the dead, you loathsome young blot?"

"The proper word is zombies," he said with defiance. "It says so in my birthday present."

He showed us his birthday present. *The Boy's Bumper Book Of Necromancy.*

Any attempt to remonstrate with the lad was cut short by the terrifying tidal wave of 'zombies' which crashed against the staircase below us. They scrambled over each other in their furious, roaring efforts to get at us, snapping their jaws and leaving bloodied handprints on the paintings hanging on the walls. Higher and higher, closer and closer they screeched!

The nearest room was, as it happened, Egbert's. We pushed a wardrobe and a chest of drawers against the door, and I braced my back against them for extra weight. The violent, relentless pounding of the mob sent shudders through me in every sense of the word.

"And what's more, you irresponsible little hound," I said to Egbert, in a tone of such severity as to shake the very foundations of human folly, "you've raised the absolute worst sort, too. Type B!"

"I dunno," shrugged Egbert, "I just did the ritual." He pointed to the carpet, where a pentagram and a generous helping of runic symbols had been drawn out in blackboard chalks.

"Can't you un-do it?" said Emerald, taking the book from him and flicking hurriedly through the pages.

"You need the next book in the series for that," said Egbert, "and I haven't got it." He sniffed and pulled up his long socks.

"Don't worry Emerald," I said, with all the gallantry I could muster, i.e. barely enough to fill an eggcup. "I'll think of something." Unfortunately, all I could think of was being murdered and eaten by those horrors out there!

Emerald held up the book, opened to a page headed 'Tomb Time!' "He's right, there's no counter-ritual! We're doomed! Those zombies will break in here any second, and if we jump out of the window we'll only land on more zombies!"

"Sir, I believe the crisis may yet have a solution," said Perkins.

"Good heavens, Perkins," I said, "are you one of those valets who moonlights as a student of the dark arts?"

"No, Sir. However, while in the employ of Governor Cottingham, shortly before I entered your service, his Excellency was much troubled by vengeful spirits. Their suppression required a working knowledge of pentagrammatical procedure. Black magic being at the root of our current zombie infestation, Sir, gives me some confidence of a similar result."

The savage buffeting from behind me was unrelenting. There was a sharp splintering sound, and I glanced up to see that the top section of the door had been bashed through. Fingers scratched loudly at the jagged hole.

"Master Egbert," said Perkins calmly, "I presume your ritual included the use of a chalice?"

"Sort of," sniffed Egbert. He rummaged around and produced a small bowl taken from the kitchens. "That stuff at the bottom is squashed beetles and worms. They were a sacrifice."

Perkins took the bowl and placed it at the centre of the pentagram. "To appease the ancient gods, and silence the evil that has been wrought, a drop of human blood must fall into the, er, receptacle."

"Fine, well, that can be Egbert's!" I said. "Go on, bleed him. Serves him right."

"Oi!" cried Egbert.

"That won't be necessary, Sir," said Perkins, producing a small penknife, "I can easily provide the required sample."

From above me came a deafening shriek! One of the undead, a decayed, stinking monstrosity, was squeezing through and grabbing wildly at me. I think I may have momentarily lost my casual *sang froid* and let out a squeak of fright.

A single, tiny red globe dripped from the end of Perkins' finger.

The effect was both immediate and startling. The zombie above me slumped, dead once more. The cacophony of screams and yells, all over the house, suddenly ceased. For half a minute or more, there was nothing but a blissful silence.

I stepped away from the wrecked door. "Gosh," I whispered.

Crisis solved. Perkins dabbed his finger with a handkerchief which he neatly returned to his top pocket; Emerald tidied her bob and kept a firm hold on that wretched book; I checked my watch and was delighted to find that I might still be in time to triumph at the Gadfly Club Darts Tournament final! Egbert glared at us sulkily.

"Perkins," I said, "you have saved the day."

"Yes," sighed Emerald, "you really are the absolute frog's whiskers."

"Thank you very much indeed, Miss."

*A*nd now the king and queen, and the little princes, and their courtiers, stared with unending terror into the nightmare of their fate. They saw what was becoming of them, their limbs and digits turning into metal tubes, articulated by hinges and socket joints. Their bodies were metal too, filled with gears and springs, wire pulleys and intricate hydraulics. Their jaws were bolted into place, to flap in imitation of human speech. Their eyes rolled on gimbals. Where their spines had been there were circular keyholes, for winding up their clockwork mechanisms.

They were automata, soon to be trapped as such forever.

"You see?" said Boneweed to the djinn. "My plan is close to completion."

Voices In The Head

One evening, not long after the wedding, he tried to explain to his wife what the voices in his head sounded like. The voices were real and came to him from outside himself, that much he knew and had proved by reasoning, but they weren't quite voices in the usual sense, as such, because their speech – more often their song – wasn't made of language. Not once, not ever in his whole life, had he heard them utter a specific, recognisable word.

He wished there was some way he could get her to hear them too. They were hard to explain and he understood why people found his wandering attention and strange listening-moods so irritating.

Whenever the cacophony of everyday noise stopped drowning out the voices for a while, whenever he could catch what they spoke – more often sang – he had to listen. He had to. Their sound was as delicate and intricate as a cobweb, a fluttering at the far edge of what was audible, sometimes harmonious and sometimes discordant but always, always hauntingly beautiful. Sometimes, a single voice would whisper its mystery but usually there were many.

He had to listen. Intently and consciously. He had to make sense of them, he would tell people, he felt compelled to decode them, to unravel their strange enigma. He would tell himself much the same, but more than anything else he was compelled to simply experience them, every day and every night, to feel the calming embrace of a loveliness to which he alone was witness. He fumbled for ways to describe these feelings to his wife.

She didn't, or couldn't, understand what he was talking about. She'd married him, in part, because she was sure her love would cure him of his shyness and his detachment, and this peculiar self-sabotaging preoccupation of his. It took her several years to finally give up and admit he was incurable, and from that moment their relationship was doomed. But then, as many observers have pointed out, wanting the impossible is the central tragedy of marriage – women want their men to change, men want their women to stay forever young.

He knew for certain that the voices weren't in his imagination because they'd been with him from as far back as he could remember, since early childhood, and any imaginative small child would have dreamed up something definite and communicative, not an ethereal muttering. Besides, after a while imagination would surely have altered or developed them in some way, or at least settled on a meaning for them, but their only variation was the slow, irregular wax and wain of their complexity.

His habitual listening caused strangers to label him in various ways: dreamer, creep, psycho, bleedin' idiot. The medical and psychological specialists who examined him as a child eventually shrugged their shoulders and let him be. In himself, he was a kind and thoughtful person, if a little serious, so his small circle of friends accepted his occasional breaking off in the middle of a conversation, or his absence-until-nudged, as mere eccentricities. He's just tuned out, they'd say with a smile.

Over the course of years he went through several distinct phases in his thoughts about the voices. The riddle of their presence was too intriguing to him to leave uninvestigated for long.

There was a religious phase. Was he hearing the voices of angels in Heaven? If so, why didn't they make themselves understandable? Why did they reveal nothing to him? Or were they the work of the Devil? But to what possible end? Quite quickly, the illogical dead weight of religious doctrine led him to abandon any ideas about divine intervention.

There was a scientific phase. Were the voices a form of tinnitus? No, it wouldn't account for their harmonies and variations. Were they caused by undiagnosed brain lesions, or tumours, or damage to his inner ears? Not according to multiple scans. He spent a long time searching medical textbooks and writing to experts in auditory neurology, but he could find no diseases or syndromes which might explain his situation.

There was a commercial phase. Could he duplicate the beauty of the voices? Could musical instruments or audio software reproduce their loveliness closely enough to create something that the whole world could hear and enjoy? Apparently not. Expensive experimentation produced little more than a trembling noise.

There was a theoretical phase. Were the voices an extra-sensory phenomenon? Was he picking up the electrical impulses of other people's brains? Perceiving thoughts from the future? Or messages from the stars? His initial enthusiasm faded into disillusion as soon as he realised any possible data hidden in the voices was so far beyond his intellectual capacity to decipher it was pointless even considering.

There was a philosophical phase. For some time, he became very interested in the Bostrom question, mulling over the concept of life being nothing but a digital simulation in which everyone – or maybe he alone! – was part of a computer-maintained illusion. Were the voices the quantum chatter of programmed subroutines? Were they the conscious stirrings of an artificial mind? He found the idea disturbing but plausible because it also explained odd-but-commonplace things as glitches in the system, things such as déjà vu, or pareidolia, or the constant vanishing of small objects from his coat pockets. However, this brought him no closer to how, and why, the voices took such a cryptic but beguiling form. In any case, the absurdly small chance of proving the simulation hypothesis one or the other in his lifetime led him to abandon this line of thought too.

From now on, he said to himself, he would make no more attempts to analyse the voices in his head. They were his unique, steadfast companion, the most constant thing in his life and he would trust them to reveal their mystery to him in their own time, if ever. He would be content to receive them.

After his wife left him, he went into a gradual but inexorable decline. Her leaving made him feel forced into making a choice between paying attention to the outside world and paying attention to the voices. It wasn't a hard choice to make. The world was nothing but noise, chaos, uncertainty, anxiety, hassle. The voices were his oasis of calm.

In time, even the most forgiving of his friends drifted away, gently pushed by his renewed dedication. He began to spend as much time as he could on the saggy, used sofa he'd bought after the divorce. He'd arrange three cushions at one end in a specific stack, then sit at the precise point to swivel and lay down into the optimum position, head on the cushions, feet on the opposite arm rest. Here he was comfortable enough to stay for as long as he wanted.

He would place his hands by his sides, relax, close his eyes and listen. In stillness, the voices became clear. They whispered in the distance but, if he lay very quiet and didn't move a muscle, they could be tempted closer like a nervous deer in the woods. Their sibilant mumblings flowed and entwined around each other, a perfect ballet of opaque debate, each voice different but in wondrous, effortless accord.

He hardly dared breathe in case he disturbed the voices' gossamer utterances. And all the time, he longed to catch a phrase, a word, a syllable, to hear a hint of meaning. There were elusive seconds, especially in the short, unpredictable moments when the voices spoke as one, when he'd feel a faint brush against his mind as if a significant connection, in a language he might grasp, was no more than a single, fleeting thought away. But then the strange harmonies would curl into intricate patterns of sound and his heart would enfold into their absolute beauty.

He would lay still on his sofa for many hours at a time, never sleeping, always attentive to the voices and always in awe of them. He would lose awareness of time passing and often opened his eyes to find that day had snapped into night or that he was suddenly cold and hungry.

Before long, he began to lose weight. His diet had become steadily worse once ease and speed were its main criteria. He grew sallow and dry-skinned, and because his ever-more-meagre resources rarely stretched to new clothes he took on a scarecrow appearance.

He had trouble finding jobs, and more trouble keeping them. He started to resent all but the most passing intrusions into his time and his innermost thoughts. Making household deliveries was work he stuck with for a while, until the demands on his dwindling energies were too much. He sold most of his furniture – not his sofa, of course – and most of his personal possessions, including the clothes that were now too large for him, and he moved the few items left into a bedsit in a cheap, seedy area of town.

He never felt bitter or upset about his unchecked slump into poverty, because the voices would always console him, soothe him, set his mind sparkling with their siren call. He could always lay on his sofa, shut out the world, and submit to the great cosmic riddle. He had no inclination to occupy himself with anything else, no desire except to listen and be fulfilled. The periods of time he spent wrapped in the voices grew longer and longer. Each return to his room, with its stained ceiling and its dusty floor, left him more exhausted, more adrift, more profoundly alone. His loneliness fed his need to listen, and his need to listen sapped everything else of colour and relevance.

Eventually, there came a grey twilight when a sudden screech from the street pulled him back to awareness and he realised he could not get up. He could move his arms and turn his head, but he couldn't sit or swing his legs aside in order to stand. He didn't have the energy any more. His strength had gone. He remembered how feeble he'd felt when he'd lay down, and how carefully he'd needed to position himself, but he had no idea he hadn't moved for several days and nights.

At first, he didn't particularly care. But soon he saw the tremor in his hands and felt the gnawing in his stomach. The edges of his small room seemed miles away. His body felt as light as a feather and as heavy as concrete. Several times he tried and failed to roll over, then lay still, frightened by his own shallow gasps. He tried to cry out, but his throat was too dry and disused to make much more than a croak.

It dawned on him that he might die. A dozen fretful, powerless hours later, with his head aching and unable to feel his feet, he was sure he would die. A darkness of loss and grief overwhelmed him. Cold fear welled up though his neglected and emaciated body.

Utterly helpless, he turned for solace to the voices in his head. His lips trembled with emotion as he focussed on their distant, quavering song. If he must face death, he thought, he would do so on his own terms. And for the briefest of moments, he almost forgot about looming, fatal shadows. The voices were comforting to him at first, but soon he became worried. His brow twitched.

They were changing, in a way so subtle and so small that only a lifetime's attentive listening could possibly have noticed it. Their tone was shifting, almost imperceptibly. For long minutes, he tried to persuade himself that his own nervousness was the only change here, but he remained unconvinced. There was the tiniest shade of urgency in the voices now, a fractional brightening which nothing less than the experience of decades told him was an expression of pleasure.

Pleasure, and gloating.

Suddenly, there was an icy hollowness inside him. After decades of opacity, of incomprehension, he construed the voices as pleased at the prospect of his death. Theirs was a muttered requiem reaching its climactic notes.

Had this been their purpose, their meaning, all along? To sing him to his grave?

He felt only fear. Had the voices been nothing but a lure? To draw him in? To intrigue and tease, to engage his senses, to absorb his time and his concentration. To drain the most precious thing in his possession, the span of his life, like wasps injecting then ingesting their prey.

He thought, with rapidly growing horror, about the countless hours he had willingly spent in thrall to the voices.

Spent. Used up, gone and irretrievable. It was too late for the acid pain of regret. His life had withered away and would soon be over.

How could it be true? How could anything so beautiful be so malevolent, so manipulative, so cruel? The voices in his head had wasted him, in every sense. His life was a husk and now he was trapped, drained and immobile, beyond rescue.

Even then, he might have reconciled himself to his fate, if only the voices had ceased. But their chatter and whisper and song were unending, and his fear burnt into ashes of horrible despair.

How long? Nothing could defeat his foolish weakness, no valiant effort of mind or body. Through the window of his room he saw the sunrise and he saw the sunset. The voices spoke their interminable mourning and every moment was a torture of twisting blades through his soul. He wanted to scream out his torment, but all he could do was listen, listen, listen. Minute after minute after minute.

Eventually, his mind drowned in anguish, he sensed the onset of death like doors being closed and locked in a darkened building. He died with no outward sign to mark his passing, and it was only with the ending of his consciousness that the voices were beyond his hearing.

His body was found one week later, when the smell from his room alerted neighbours. They found him on the sofa, his eyes staring in terror, his hands clawed as if warding off something unrelenting and evil.

The storm roared and thundered, as if applauding the grotesque tableau that was now complete inside the castle. Nothing stirred, nor ever would again, for there were no keys to insert into the silent ranks of automata, no way to set their clockwork in motion. Their happy painted faces would never change.

The braziers would soon burn out and the ballroom would go dark and cold. The citizens of the Inner Realms would quickly abandon the place and its cursed inhabitants, and the castle would become the haunt of fearful lore. Thus, centuries would pass.

And inside each automaton, a soul screamed forever.

Boneweed slipped a final parchment from a pile on his cart. The djinn, in its iron and glass prison, flowed faster.

"I set the seal upon this dark enchantment," whispered Boneweed, touching the bars of the cage, "to set you free..."

Skincrawler

I've never liked my face, so the idea of cutting something off it never struck me as anything peculiar. I avoid looking at my reflection wherever possible, and the only actual mirror I possess is the small one in my bathroom, a rectangular metal thing on a pivoting base. I don't even like catching a glimpse of myself, fleetingly, full length, in the swing of a glass door or in a shiny shopfront because the rest of me isn't exactly impressive either. Not quite as bad as what's above the collar, but nothing of any interest.

My face is in a league of its own. From top to bottom: my hair is lank and thin, a nondescript semi-brown, and I would have shaved it all off years ago if my head wasn't a lumpy Neanderthal horror; my forehead is a patchwork of lines and nastily textured areas; without a weekly trim, my eyebrows would be grotesque caterpillars staring at each other over a hairy valley; my eyes are piss holes in the snow, close enough together for people to say "his eyes are too close together" without fear of contradiction; my nose is a vast, jutting triangle of flesh, easily large enough to have its own gravitational pull (which might account for the eye closeness, now I come to think of it); my cheeks are a wasteland of blotches and pores which manage to look both roseate and unhealthily pallid at the same time; my mouth is distractingly wide and gash-like, made worse by lips which look like slices of raw liver; the less said about my weak chin the better – or rather chins, plural, since fat's first choice of residence on my body is around my neck.

I've tried hiding as much of myself as possible behind various types of beard, and distracting from the overall effect with glasses of different shapes and sizes, but none of it really helped. I look like someone who's been dropped head first into industrial machinery, and that's that. A face to frighten horses, badly assembled by blind chimpanzees on a roller coaster. Nothing more to be said.

I should add, I look nothing like my parents. My father was ruggedly handsome and my mother was positively beautiful, so the only blame falls to life's genetic lottery. I managed to retain a kind of gnome-ish cuteness through my childhood, which spared me from too much visual peer review, but once the hormones kicked in I blossomed like a Venus fly trap or one of those smelly toadstools.

Which is why, when one day I felt a little puckered lump on my right cheek, level with my cheekbone, I was having none of it. My face was bad enough already, without further shite trying to muscle in!

The lump was soft, roughly oval, about six or seven millimetres across. Definitely not a wart, not seborrhoeic, not angry enough to be a cancer. Not smooth, like a lipoma or a cyst. Not in a cluster, not a rash. Just skin which had decided to erupt a bit. To annoy me. To disfigure me. Or rather, disfigure me more.

It was flattish, with a patterned top surface. I dabbed a bit of ink on it and rubbed, so the pattern would show more clearly. Kind of crackled, like the bed of a dried lake. I washed the ink away.

I'm not having this, I said to myself. It crossed my mind to remove it with sandpaper or to file it away with a shaving razor, but quickly realised neither of these would work. You need the right tools for the right job, so I bought a proper scalpel, a No.3 handle with a supply of No.11 carbon steel surgical blades seemed to fit the bill. A nice straight cutting edge, with a sharp tip for lancing.

I sat on the end of the bath and leaned forward over the wash basin. I set the mirror down between the taps and angled it so I could get a good, close view of the bastard. Tipping my head to one side, so that the light from the bathroom window shone directly onto my cheek, I pulled the skin over my cheekbone tight with one hand and wielded the scalpel with the other.

Scape, or cut? There'd probably be blood, but how much? Somewhere between a tiny dot and a fire hose jet, it was impossible to say. An exploratory scrape.

I felt the skin pull a little, but the blade was very sharp and took off the top of the pattern. It was a second or two before half a dozen pinpricks of red slowly swelled and pooled into a droplet. I soaked it away with a fold of loo paper. After a minute or so, the blood had settled into a brown crust and I took a second go at it.

I was firmer this time, keeping the blade pressed to flat background skin, scraping down in a short, single movement. There was more blood this time, enough to drip once, twice into the basin. I left a little rip of tissue glued over it for half an hour, like a shaving nick, and when I cleaned it up and re-examined the area I was delighted to see that all that was left was my normal, hideous cheek.

Success! The scraping was a bit pinker than the surrounding area, but it'd settle down.

And it did, within a few days. An almost invisible repair. I thought no more about it until a second one appeared, a couple of weeks later. This one was on my forehead, above my left eye. It was bigger, about a centimetre in diameter, but protruded no more than the first. It felt rough beneath the touch of my fingertip.

I assumed the Bathroom Position and removed it in two efficient scrapes, as before. This time there was a little more blood, and half way through the second cut I had to put my head forward to avoid a rivulet running into my eye. Keeping my head still, I groped for the toilet roll and unravelled a small wad.

Success again. Not quite as undetectable a removal as the first time, but infinitely better than letting the little fucker pitch camp on my land.

It was the following month when half a dozen little fuckers invaded the same territory. These were different, more like firm nodules, which were no more than a couple of millimetres across and which appeared to be vaguely cylindrical in shape. I dug out a magnifying glass and spent several minutes adjusting the mirror and my angle of view so that I could get a close look. There were seven of them in all, arranged in no discernable formation. Each was indeed more or less cylindrical, as if tiny circles of skin had risen up vertically by about half a centimetre.

Out came the scalpel. They barely bled at all. It was with great pleasure than I looked down into the basin to see all seven, neatly severed, clinging to the porcelain by drips of moisture. A quick swirl from the cold tap took care of them. Arrgh, glug, help. So perish all invaders.

To my intense annoyance, they left behind minute blemishes on my forehead, like fly turds on a window. Only visible close up, amid the general Somme-like facial landscape, so the only person who would ever really see them was me, but irritating none the less. It made me feel that my victory was incomplete.

Then, as if the inhabitants of Little Fuckertown had mourned their dead and declared war, another batch appeared. Each one twice the size, this time, and twice the length. One on my forehead, near the hairline, three clustered on the outer orbital of my right eye, three more about four centimetres below, on my cheek, and one on the side of my nose. The invasion took place overnight. Sneaky.

I considered seeking medical help, if only because of the rapidity of the attack. In the end, I decided against it, because I knew there was nothing Dr Swan at Hilltop Medical Centre could possibly tell me, or prescribe me, that would deal with the situation quickly and decisively. Oh, just an ageing thing, he'd say, simple EBV infection, routine skin tags, perfectly harmless, clear up of its own accord in time, creams from the pharmacy, or put a bit of crushed garlic on them at night, that often shrinks them in a month or two. No help at all. Besides, I wouldn't be able to hide them completely when in public, even if I wore a cough mask. No, I thought, a home remedy would be best.

Several of them were at awkward angles. Once I'd sliced them away – very little blood again, fortunately – I found I had to have another go at them the next day, to clear up leftover wedges and crescents. The nose one left spurs I could only remove by snipping at them with a pair of nail clippers.

I'd got through five blades by this point. They didn't keep maximum sharpness for long, and once they'd touched blood I preferred to dispose of them rather than attempt sterilisation.

The marks left were more noticeable this time. I was thoroughly pissed off.

But not nearly as pissed off as I was some days later, when it was obvious that another battalion of little fuckers were charging for freedom. They came with allies. Rough buggers similar to the first two I'd removed, but more florid, as if the sweat from strategically chosen pores had suddenly fountained and frozen into flesh.

I watched them all develop for 48 hours – luckily it was the weekend and I could stay inside – until they'd evidently done their worst and I could stand the sight of them no longer. I resolved to eliminate them all in one fell swoop and tidy up afterwards.

I set to work. It took a while, partly because there were more of them and partly because the fleshy ones seemed to be filled with capillaries this time. Red ran down my face like battle scars. Some dripped off my chin into the sink, some dribbled down the folds of my neck and stained the collar of my shirt, which exasperated me into redoubling my efforts.

I experimented with grasping the nodules in a pair of tweezers and then pulling my skin out into a cone shape, to give myself a clearer point at which to cut. This worked well and I used the method on the fleshy ones too.

Once I'd finished, my face was striped and smeared with blood. The downward inner curve of the wash basin looked as if some sort of embryonic mammal had been hacked limb from limb. The skin tingled at every location I'd snipped.

Later, with everything cleaned and dried, I was furious at the blemishes every last one of the little fuckers had left behind. Parts of my face looked like the surface of the bloody Moon! I gave these blemishes one week to improve. They resolutely would not.

And so, thinking back to my earliest, more tentative excisions, it was clear that the thing to do would be to scrape away a layer or two of surface skin around the affected areas, in order to remove all traces of these discoloured shapes. I fitted a fresh blade to my scalpel.

Now I was being a bit more stringent than before, the scraping action tended to sting sharply. Here and there, I inadvertently made it worse by misjudging the pressure needed and breaking the skin rather than thinning it. Trickles of blood welled up from the resulting narrow slits. However, I soon became proficient at the correct technique.

I left things overnight and re-examined the battlefield in the morning. The overall effect of the scraping was quite stark, with raggedly delineated rectangles in a darker shade than everything around them. Garish, colour-wise but – to my delight – absolutely smooth. I was completely confident that once the scraped skin was back to its normal thickness, it would be as if the little fuckers had never existed. The stinging would fade as the new layers grew.

I was right, more or less. On the plus side, the itchiness subsided and the little fuckers had indeed been erased completely. On the minus side, the scraped skin had, if anything, become slightly lighter in tone than before. Which didn't make any sense to me whatsoever.

The next task, then, was to even everything out. It only occurred to me as I was sitting down in front of the mirror, getting ready, that here was an unexpected opportunity. Hadn't I bemoaned the patchy, blotchy, muddy field quality of my skin a thousand times? Weren't those craters and rough areas part and parcel of the entire problem? Of course they were! And now, in tending to one short-term problem I could be dealing with dozens of long-term ones too!

Why the hell hadn't I thought of this before? It was as if I'd spent years eating bloody horrible porridge and then suddenly plopped a blob of strawberry jam into it without even thinking. I snorted out a loud stream of laughter, shaking my head in disbelief.

Another fresh blade, and I set to work with a skip in my heart. To remove layers from every square centimetre of face took a long time. Towards the end, I had to pause to pull the bathroom light cord, then re-adjust my position relative to the mirror to catch the overhead glow properly. I dripped on the lino, going back and forth, and tutted crossly to myself. Should have put down a couple of towels.

At long last the job was done. Cleaning up took ages. Rather than wash them away, I scooped all the bits of removed skin out of the basin using wraps of loo paper, in case they clogged the U-bend under the plug hole. They flushed away without any bother. The blobs on the lino needed to be thoroughly scrubbed, however.

The rawness of my face felt very burn-y and prickly. I applied some gauze, which I found I needed to refresh every couple of hours because sections of skin would unhelpfully decide to leak again, or turn watery. It got worse before it got better, but eventually pulled itself together. Once it was dry and settled, I was able to patrol my handiwork in detail.

Though I say so myself, I'd done a pretty good job. Close up, some edges were visible where the results of my first thinning session met the second, but these were faint enough not to cause me any undue concern. Much of the skin's delicate surface, when touched, crumpled inwards slightly, as if I was pressing the cellophane on a packet of something. It felt taught and scintillant, like bees buzzing. Unwilling to encourage further inflammation, I decided to leave my facial hair unattended for a while.

What did cause me concern was my nose. The varying angles and lines of sight I'd needed to use had left it in something of a state. Unfortunately, the smoothness I'd achieved on all the surrounding tissue simply highlighted the misshapen, doughy appearance of the nose itself. Naturally, I realised that re-moulding it, to balance it out and reduce its gargantuan size, would leave a certain amount of scarring. I um'd and er'd for a while, weighing up the pros and cons, and came to the conclusion that some scarring on an adjusted nose was better than a nose left to look like this.

I ran the cold water tap while I cut, to swoosh away blood as I went along instead of leaving it until I'd finished, and I placed a sieve in the basin to catch slices of skin, cartilage and muscle. I put a pile of towels within arm's reach, just in case.

I have to say, it hurt quite a lot. What was most irritating was that the constant flow of blood made it really difficult to make sure I was taking the same amount off both sides. This was especially important when it came to the tip, since discrepancies would stick out like the proverbial sore thumb! In the end, I had to take several extra bits off before I was happy.

By now, the mental concentration involved was making me feel exhausted, so I rested for a while. I wrapped a bath towel around my head and had a glass of water and a lie-down.

Waking refreshed, I washed away as much of the dried blood as I could and put the towel in the laundry basket. My nose was triumphantly transformed from rocky mountain to gentle hillock, a great relief in itself, but it was a triumph spoiled from above by the ghastly overhang of my brow, and from below by the rolling excrescence of my neck fat.

Getting rid of both was messy but surprisingly straightforward. I made the silly mistake of tackling my brow first, which meant I was constantly fighting to stop my eyes swamping-up with blood, but apart from that everything went well. It took only a few deft slices to make the brow acceptably flatter, although I was conscious that there was bone relatively close to the surface here. I had to cut with one hand and push sideways at the flesh with the other, to prevent it bunching and sending the blade off course.

Dealing with the neck fat was actually rather fun. Once I'd properly gauged the depth at which the fat ended and the musculature began, it was like carving up a Sunday roast or chopping tomatoes. By raising my chin and pulling my neck taut the task became a simple case of keeping the carving action nice and steady. Which wasn't always easy, because the amount of blood was considerable and the peeling sensation left behind by the scalpel became really harsh and uncomfortable. Now and again, my fingers started to shake – no gain without pain, I said to myself.

With towels finally wrapped in place, I suddenly found I had carelessly allowed my clothes to get completely soaked with blood. I had to stand in the bath to take them all off, otherwise I'd have splattered half the bathroom! I must have been feeling a bit brain-swimmy because I distinctly remember wondering whether to put my trousers in the laundry basket or just bin them instead.

Thinking about it, I must have been more than a bit brain-swimmy, because I managed to forget all about the bathroom sink until the next day, or it may have been the day after that. I walked in and stopped dead when I realised I'd left stains all over the basin and the taps, although I had to laugh at the sight of all the fat strips collected at the bottom, like a bowl of spaghetti bolognese made by a ham-fisted chef!

Anyway, at first, I was quite nervous about exhibiting my new look in public. I knew that the changes I'd made were immediately noticeable – why else make them at all, for fuck's sake? – and on the one hand I didn't want anyone feeling forced to saying something positive but, on the other hand, feeling they couldn't say anything for fear of embarrassment. I wasn't sure which reaction was worse! I understood how it must feel to go out wearing a hairpiece for the first time, or misjudge your teeth whitening.

In the end, I needn't have worried. People stared, naturally, because I looked radically different. People gawp and turn away, or subconsciously move their children aside, but nothing I haven't been used to my entire adult life. And I feel such renewed confidence, in myself, in my heart of hearts, an inner strength I never knew I had. This is me.

I'm much happier with my face now. This is a vast improvement.

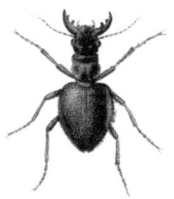

The cracking of the thick glass inside the djinn's prison cage echoed off the vaulted ceiling, louder than cannon fire. Boneweed's heart raced as he watched the djinn seep from the cracks in a nebulous tumult of curves and formulae.

It coalesced into a nearly-shape which glittered in deep reds and purples. It throbbed as if stretching many arms and legs, and the air was filled with vibrations so forceful they made Boneweed's eyes pulse and his teeth jitter.

He raised his arms. "I set you free!" he breathed.

The djinn's voice was made from sounds of loneliness and dread. "Your service has been true to me. I gift you wishes without guile."

"I ask only one," said Boneweed, trembling with emotion. He hurried over to his cart. "I care not for myself but, I beg you, please, preserve the library to which I have dedicated my life. Hundreds of tales have I gathered here, precious remnants of unknown pasts and futures. Let them survive. Give meaning to my curation of them. Give them to the Universe, to every reality! Give them life!"

"It is so," said the Djinn Of Continuum.